Message from the High Inquest

Speeding Towards the End of ... What?

As of this third issue of *Inquestor Tales*, it looks like I'm about three-quarters of the way through a book, and that book looks increasingly like part one of a trilogy. Or at the very least, a "dilogy". Sounds a bit filthy, eh? Bilogy? "Duology" is a word I've seen sometimes, but etymologically it's a bit uncomfortable. It's clear, anyway, that Sajit's side story may end up being told in more than one book.

Could the Inquestors series, three decades later, suddenly spawn a whole new spinoff trilogy? I had thought, perhaps one book about the childhood of Sajit, and one book about how the High Inquest came to be, centering on the Lady Varuneh.

In other words, I was thinking of doing two more books, one because so many mysteries are hinted at in the series already about the origins of the High Inquest — but I did not myself know the answers — the other because the character of Sajit, the perpertual outsider who watches history unfold with clear-eyed *gravitas*, has always been one I felt deeply sympathetic to.

More sympathetic than normal, even. Perhaps, on some level, I see myself in this character. Someone so conflicted in identity as to sometimes fracture into two (or more) individuals. Someone who has moved from civilization to civilization during a curious, eventful childhood.

I noticed that I have something in common with one of my childhood idols, Chip Delany (Samuel R., that is) — which is that when I started publishing, my protagonists tended to be about ten years younger than me, but as I aged, they did, too. In writing about Sajit I seem to have returned to my own beginnings, though I seem to be looking at them from a old man's viewpoint. It's strange.

I never dreamed that Sajit would split into two. It happened when the character took on a life of its own, much different from the flashbacks and brief descriptions mentioned in the 1980s tales of the High Inquest.

In those stories, Sajit was a child of a slum: today he would be sniffing glue or fleecing tourists in some huge, vaguely oriental-bazaar-like city. But when I started writing this novel, there was a Sajit with a completely different background, and a completely unconnected childhood, yet I recogized that this childhood was a true as the random snippets that have existed for forty years (the Inquestor Universe first surfaced in *Analog* in 1979, so that's really how old it is).

Not only did I have to write about this childhood while not rendering the previous stories un-canon — I had to reconcile the more than one past — find out how they became one *person's* past.

And that, you see, is why this story while take longer than one novel. Because it has to happen without time travel or alternate histories. I can't cheat.

Okay I can, but only when making the rules; once the rules are in place, there's no more cheating....

— Somtow

INQUESTOR TALES

Despatches from the High Inquest • Number Three •
May, 2019
Diplodocus Press • Bangkok • Los Angeles

—

Contents

ISBN: 978-1-94099939-5
Diplodocus Press
Bangkok • Los Angeles
www.diplodocuspress.com

Questioning Mr. Khashoggi

a sonnet

We flew to Turkey, all fifteen of us,
On different flights; that way the chance decreases
Of all those nosy spies making a fuss.
But what the hell? The man just went to pieces
When all we did was try to question him.
He'd had a soft life in the U.S.A.
So a plain hacksaw could remove a limb,
A puny squeeze turn quick flesh into clay.
Amp up the music to drown out the screams,
For "freedom" is a mantra for the weak —
Throttle one throat and quash a thousand dreams!
A child in Yemen's tougher than this geek.
You want a visa for your future wife? —
The fees are steep — it's going to cost — your life.

S.P. Somtow

CHRONICLES OF THE HIGH INQUEST
The Homeworld of the Heart

by S.P. Somtow

Book Three
THE CHILD COLLECTOR

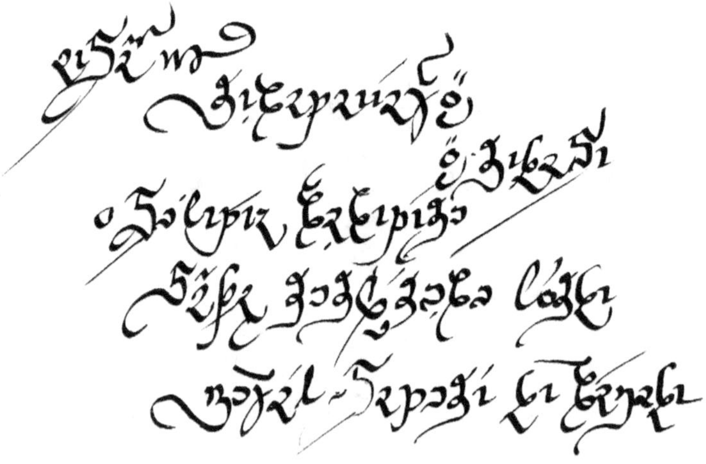

aiváh! aiváh!
kindarayághor or-kitávi
uraná vrendáh
u velirís dhandiríske
vãzhas kekýrkende lukti
meghal-vareký ti dhánati

He comes! He comes!
The child collector with his golden scroll!
He'll take you to the sky
Where you'll fly, where you'll die
spinning disks of light,
with your lightning eyes of death.

— traditional

Interlude
Elloran

Ton Elloran n'Taanyel Tath dreamed:

Stairs, stairs, carved into a mountain, stairs twisting, coiling; stairs broken and overgrown with scarlet lichen, with feathery blue moss; stairs that seemed to move as he ascended, changing direction, studded with random displacement disks; and he climbed. Not as a powerful Inquestor, older than time yet as vigorously preserved as the finest thinkhives could preserve, constantly monitoring his every heartbeat even from uncountable parsecs away ... no, old as a shortliver is old, wheezing, with a cane that slipped and skidded on the uneven stones.

How long did the dream go on?

He could not tell. The steps kept going. Up, up, left, round, sideways, right, wrong. broken; he would never reach the top ... the more he hurries, the more steps there are ... but at last he is standing in a place where many rainbows meet. A windy place near the summit, where rainbows fall like drifting ribbons in the wind.

And there she is ... he knows he will find her ... a young girl standing there. She is drapped in rainbows. And she says, again and again, *Do you remember?* but though he hears her speak, her lips do not move.

And he say to her, *Kerin.*

Sister, he says. *Sister.*

In the dream she has not changed, though in reality she must be long gone, stranded in an unreachable past; if he has changed, she must have changed infinitely more; time dilation takes its toll on the shortlived.

Enguester eis, she whispers. *Mun ma'vendek dáve, evendek bhratek.*

And you will always be my little sister, Kerin, Elloran says. *But why are we meeting now? Shouldn't you be gone by now, forever gone?* He wonders why she speaks the Highspeech because when they were children together it was not the language they chose, not the language of intimacy.

Kerin laughs. The lips move but the sound, the lips, are not together, as though sound and light are travelling through diverging streams of spacetime.

In the land where I dwell, she says, *even the beggars speak* Bhasháhokh, *because it is the true speech, the language where words have souls.*

Elloran does not have to ask her where she lives. Only one world in the cosmos has this sky.

It is Uran s'Varek, which is what many people call *heaven,* but which only Inquestors know to be a real place — a place forbidden to the shortlived, known to them only in legend —

For looking up from the summit of the mountain, he sees where he is standing in this dream —

The sky of Uran s'Varek is only to be experienced, never spoken of. Imagine a world that is a sphere, built millions of years ago around the black hole at the galaxy's heart. Imagine a cubic parsec of space that contains packed within it uncountable stars. Imagine an attenuated atmosphere rising thousands of klomets, enough to scatter all that light and shield all that radiation. Imagine the perpetual light. No night. Just the pearly, soft, ineffable radiance of almost two million suns.

All kept together by the will of a single thinkhive.

Do you believe in heaven, Loreh? Kerin says. *Is heaven just a dream the Inquestors made, to keep the million worlds in balance, to keep the Dispersal of Man obedient and docile?*

If she were only real....

Embrace me, bhratek. Then you'll know how real I am.

In the warmth of that embrace, Ton Elloran n'Taanyel Tath has a fleeting idea he can barely grasp ...

First, the great thinkhive of Uran s'Varek. A mind greater than any species can imagine, natural or artificial no one knows — *and still evolving.*

Could it be that Kerin's thought patterns have been absorbed into the all-embracing matrices of the great thinkhive of Uran s'Varek ... could she still be alive in some form ... at least in dreams?

You're so real —

Of course I am. Why wouldn't I be?

Could it be that the thinkhive of Uran s'Varek *is* heaven? Could it be that every thought ever thought, every dream dreamed, every song sung, is forever part of the thinkhive, as it finds new connections in the chaos.

Is the myth of a human soul real, and do souls migrate to heaven?

Kerin laughs.

We were matched twins, she says. *We should have grown up together. We were destined from birth to share throne and bed, to be left and right, up and down, to dance perpetually hand in hand around the center of light....*

There are *no ghosts!* cries Elloran.

But if the thinkhive of Uran s'Varek were to contain within it the thought patterns of every person since Mother Vara awakened the world to light —

Elloran aches. He hugs his sister hard, but already she is beginning to waver, to dissolve into the everlasting daylight ...

And woke....

... clutching the whisperlyre.

How could it have known, this instrument of dead metal and rotten wood?

He would have flung it across the room. But he held back. An Inquestor does not show emotion.

Oh Sajit! Oh Tijas! If I had only known the secret we shared ... for we both had a twin we loved more than our own self ... a twin bound to us by flesh and by emotion ... an other half we with whom we would never be united .... lost in time....

***

Tash Toléon had been waiting in the antechamber. He looked up anxiously as the door dissolved.

"Tash Toléon," Elloran said, "I've had such a dream."

"Hokh'Ton, that's a very special room," Toléon said.

"Is it?" Elloran said. "Is it haunted?" He laughed bitterly. "I've spent many a night in a haunted room on a backworld. The dead never came to me — unless it was to serve my morning *zúl*. But in my dream, I saw, I saw —"

"Let me show you, my Lord."

He led the Inquestor back into the chamber. The bedfloat was draped in sheets of comforting darkness. Toléon yanked away the darkness and deopaqued the bedframe, and Elloran saw that under the bed there was a scarred wooden box.

"It's —"

"Yes, Hokh'Ton. It is the doppling kit. Still good for a few more charges, I would think, though no one has touched it in generations. There is something of Shen Sajit in the box. An essence."

"Toléon, tell me more about the two Sajits, the one I know so well, the one I never knew."

"But do you know, my Lord, which one is *your* Sajit?"

"I confess ... I know not."

Ten

The Silence Between the Stars

In a stone-arched cloister, brand new and still uninhabited, Arbát was retraining Sajit's voice; though he did not realize that it was actually Tijas's. The air was still and cold but Tijas stood shirtless, and Arbát laid his palm firmly on the boy's diaphragm, and with the other hand he made an expulsive gesture from his lips — and said over and over, "Work the air. Make the air move. Make the air vibrate."

Tijas worked his diaphragm against his teacher's relentless pressure. He hated the flaky, gnarled hand against his flat, smooth flesh. And still he was wondering where Sajit was. His whole body was still aching from the blast of agony that had reached out to him from he knew not where.

"You're drifting!" Arbát slapped his arm. "Concentrate. Now, make a tone. Shi ... shi ..."

Shirenzhá.

Silence.

"So many songs," Arbát said, "start with some variation of *shirenzhe*. Do you know why?"

"Because ..." Tijas had an inspiration ... "because *all* music begins and ends in silence."

"Find your silence," Arbát said, "and in that silence, hear your song begin."

A song began to form:

Shirenzhá in-dárein
Shirénzhen chítarans tinjáte

In the silence between the stars
Feel the silence of the heart....

The *sh* of the first word emerged from the emptiness like a surf's sussurus, a breeze, a sigh. From the *sh* sound came the *i*, a faint wuthering that grew to a ghostly wail over the course of a long melisma. *Ren* resounded; *zhá* was an explosion and *in-dárein* was a whole galaxy in a few seconds.

"You clever little beast!" Arbát said. "And all that out of a moment of silence!"

"My voice," Tijas said, "is it coming?"

"I daresay." Arbát let go of his diaphragm, held the boy by his shoulders. "It's odd ... you almost feel like someone else."

"I'm only trying to learn, Master Arbát," Tijas said, trying to sound inconspicuous.

He didn't want to show Arbát his pain. For he had not seen Sajit for several sleeps. And he found it hard to get to sleep at night without his other self beside him.

***

Most of Nevéqilas was dead, or starting to decay, riven in twain by the crashed people bin. Here and there though, the palace could still draw energy, though one could not tell where from. There were chambers that functioned as in the old days, though some could only be reached through a tangle of tunnels, or by wrongly sequenced displacement plates. And so was the apartment that Sajit's new mother wanted him to call home. The room was connected to the Temple of Aërat by a tunnel and four displacements. Éluma had never been, and rarely even *seen* a mother, but she had good instincts and she knew Sajit for her own. There was a deep bond, a real bond, though Sajit could see she needed help in playing out her role. Having given him up once, she did not quite know how to handle him. Perhaps she felt closest to him when he slept.

She would watch him, nestled in a cushion of wind, and she could see that he hard trouble sleeping. She wondered whether he thought about his other parents, his other family.

***

A few sleeps, perhaps a tennight, had passed since Orifec had returned. And Sajit felt a growing dread.

He didn't dare even to say Tijas's name in front of his mother. And he was rarely alone with his father.

Orifec still played at being a Princeling, though his kingdom was now a tiny square of land. So he usually was away somewhere — vaguely muttering about affairs of state when he came back — staying very briefly, usually not even the night.

Sajit said to Éluma after a tennight, "I have to get back to my music."

She said, "Not now, Sajitteh. Plenty of time after ... after ... you know." The time was coming. No one would say when, perhaps no one knew. "You can't be seen," Éluma said. "Don't go out."

"No, no ... *mother*. I *must* get back."

The title was torn with difficulty from his lips. It was awkward enough that his father was a king; harder still, that his mother was a goddess.

"Sajitteh ... *he* is coming. *He* whose word even a Princeling, or a Goddess, cannot resist."

***

"Who is coming?" Tijas asked, because they didn't seem to want him on the show. The Professor was distant, and Daro kept smiling and strained, pinched smile. "Why can't I go and play the prelude at least?"

Zelma says, "It's best you stay inside. Where is your twin?"

"I don't know. He went to find our mother ... *his* mother. And now ... he is missing."

"You can't go looking for him now."

"Why not? I *need* him!"

No one could understand the depth of this need. I need him, he thought, like my left hand needs my right hand. "No," Daro said. "No children in the streets, not now. *He* will soon be here."

And by *he* was meant a member of the Clan of Kyar. The child collectors. Servants of the High Inquest, architects of the culling.

"There may be a reason your doppling cannot be found," Daro said. "It is wrong to think it, perhaps. But if they have collected him ...."

"Then I'd be safe."

That was the only reason Tijas existed. To be

childsoldier in Sajit's stead.   But Sajit had not been taken.   If he were gone, there would be an emptiness. But there was no emptiness.   There was the screaming, distant, insistent.   Coloring all his thoughts.

A tennight had passed and Tijas still felt his doppling's screaming.   If he focused, he could almost feel a direction.   He knew he could find Sajit.   If he held his breath, if he made his mind go blank, there was a still unwavering point of light there.   His center, his self.

***

But outside, in the great collided city that was Aírang, there were no children in the streets.

At the edge of the star system, a delphinoid breached the overcosm.

Most of the passengers were in stasis, but one person stood on the deck when the walls deopaqued in the split second that the light-mad overcosm ended its display, the dizzying cacophony of light that drove men mad.

Even that split was almost too much to bear, though within the threshold of human endurance.   But the ship's guest of honor had learned to tolerate the crazed kaleidoscope.   In a sense, he even enjoyed it.

The ship's pilot, Kail Kruspar, entered quickly. "Lord, you shouldn't expose yourself to it," he said.

"It drives men mad, yes, yes, I know," said Kyar Gharém, Inquestral Child Collector for the sector. "I've kept my eyes closed."

Gharém had emerged from amiosis a little ahead of schedule because an alarm had triggered the awakening. Something was not quite right with the schedule — which rarely happened, despite the caprices of time dilation, for the High Inquest is frozen eternally in the space between *history* and *not-history*. The Great Thinkhive of Uran s'Varek, guardian of every sentient thought in the Dispersal of Man, did not err.

To err, however, was always possible for a human, even for an Inquestor.

Of course, he had settled down in his berth only minutes before, in his own memory, before being cast into amniosis. Within the overcosm itself, time and space had no meaning, and all events and places were coiled in amongst themselves. So: a minute later, awoken, with a message disk on the float beside his arm.

Gharém had pressed the message disk to his forehead and already seen the news.

Now, in the deck, he turned to the pilot. "Did you receive the same message?" he said.

"Yes. There has been ... a mishap in timing."

"Those cursed Inquestors!" Gharém said, shocking the pilot, who was not used to hearing the gods themselves insulted. "It's a overlapping *makrúgh.*"

"My Lord, I'm not even quite sure what that is."

"Quiet. Awaken my equerry."

But his equerry was already emerging from the tube that spiralled to the resting quarters of the delphinoid. A sharp-faced childsoldier with a squealing voice, intelligent, impertinent. "I would think you'd be eager to visit this world, Mikkálu-without-a-Clan. Weren't you born here?"

"All that is erased, Lord Collector, when one enters

the training college at Bellares. I am an empty vessel, ready to be filled by —"

"Any command of the High Inquest, yes, yes ... spare me the rote-learned platitudes, boy."

Instead of sinking into subservience mode, the boy laughed. "My Lord, I *was* born on this world," he said. "I had friends there. I grew up in a temple of the love goddess. Some would call it a brothel."

"If there were any children you grew up with," said the Child Collector, "they are older than you now. You have traveled the space between spaces."

"I'll gladly give you the grand tour, my Lord," meeting the Child Collector's gaze almost brazenly. Gharém thought, *It's true what they say, then: you can remove the whore from the brothel, but you can't ...*

"You're pensive, Lord Gharém."

"I asked for an equerry from the planet I have been assigned to collect," Gharém said, "but you don't seem entirely housebroken. Should I have you beaten?"

"If that is what you fancy, my Lord."

"Insolence!" He raised his hand to slap the child, but but held in his temper at the last minute, so that it seemed almost a fatherly pat on the cheek. The boy giggled. "Don't fidget. I have something serious to tell you. And there is no need to flirt. I prefer servocorpses; compliant, indefatigable, and uncomplaining."

"I accept the chiding from your lips, my Lord," said Mikkálu. "I'll be good now."

"Your world has been caught up in an anomaly in *makrúgh*," Gharém said. "You cannot, of course, hope to understand that, but the Dispersal of Man is kept in perpetual balance because of *makrúgh,* the game played by the High Inquestors. During the course of a game of *makrúgh,* planets may *fall beyond,* but in its compassion the High Inquest saves as much of the population as it can, keeping millions of citizens in stasis in people bins that can be released to populate worlds that have been emptied by *falling beyond.* The unthinkable has happened to your homeworld. It was simultaneously played in two different games of *makrúgh,* with overlapping outcomes. That *never* happens. There are so many worlds, and not many Inquestors."

"So my world is gone?"

"No. But it is as though a different world has grown up overnight on top of the old one. And it is the old world from which we must collect our children, Mikkálu. For when we left Bellares with this assignment, your world was still intact, and no Inquestor has commanded that I abort my mission. Not to obey would be unthinkable."

"But an error of *makrúgh* is unthinkable too, isn't it, my Lord?" the boy said, aggravating in his insistence on pointing out the imperfection.

"We shall therefore collect all the children in the lists provided by the planetary thinkhive, identifying them by their genetic signature and assembling them all for transport in the … park beside the Lake of Luminous Loons," Gharém continued, trying to ignore the boy, "assuming, of course, that the park is still there."

***

Daro said, "there's a commotion.   In the street outside."

Tijas had been holed up in the zul storeroom for many sleeps now. He knew Sajit was still in the world, in the city. He felt it.   The storeroom was not as crowded as it had been at first; many members of the troupe had found other basements, other storerooms, mostly in the same building or buildings nearby. After the initial frenzy of construction, the new Alykh was settling in and no new structures had been thrown up for at least two tennights.

"Come," Daro said.   "The Professor found a place where we can spy on the outside."

Daro led Tijas to a stairwell, overgrown with *zul-weed*.   The steps, dozens of them, curved round and round and you could walk up them by holding on to a metallic railing — more ancient technology, and like the doorknobs, cold to the touch.

The emerged in an upper room.

The Professor was working at a thinkhive nexus. She was waving her hands and lines of light and arcane formulae and patterns were materializing in the dusty air.

"Tijas," she said.   "We have to think about how to hide you...."

On one wall were screens through which one could see the street.   They were looking down on an avenue and there was a crowd.   You could hear the crowd chattering, even through the walls.   Then the crowd seemed to part and a line of childsoldiers was marching, leaping, somersaulting, shooting lines of light from topaz-colored eyes, lines that wove brilliant yellow nets of light in the darkening sky.

They shouted the bloodcurdling warcry of the childsoldiers:

Ishá ha! Ishá ha! Ishá ha ha hé ha!

There came a voice, booming beneath the descant of the warcries:

Children of Urna! Your destiny has arrived!

The Inquest calls you to Bellares, the world where children learn the art of war. Honour calls you! Blood calls you! The High Inquest summons you!

The voice came from speaker cells mounted on floating vehicles, rotating on crystalline stalks.

Your DNA has been recorded in the memories of the planetary thinkhive. Only the most perfect are chosen and it has been your destiny since birth.

Do not think to escape. We shall be releasing Finder Birds into the skies of Urna. If you are living, they shall sniff you out.

There were children in the street, Tijas saw, but they were dressed in the style of Alykh.

"Alykh isn't affected," he said. "Couldn't I just—"

"Put on Alykhish dress? No. The finding birds — they were engineered to screen out DNA — one bird per genemap — and there's a bird with your signature on it — yours — and also —"

"Sajit's!"

"One of you will *have* to go. Or you will both be in hiding forever," Zelma said.

"But your doppling is gone. For all we know, he has already been collected," Daro said. "If that's true, you will free go out. You will be free — for the rest of your life."

"Although," Zelma said, "it will blow your chance for a Clan Name. Childsoldiers who survive are among the likeliest citizens of the Dispersal to be bestowed one. Don't you want to belong to the Clan of Shen?"

Outside, the resonant announcement echoed. *This is your destiny! Honor calls you! Blood calls you! Ishá ha!*

The view made him nervous. Tijas subvocalized the universal command for opaquing a wall. But nothing happened. He stood in front of the screens, blinking.

The Professor started to laugh. "It's not a normal wall," she said. "Those are windows. *Real* windows. See? Try knocking on one."

He did. There was a crystalline, brittle sound. He realized that it was actually a clear material, not a programmable wall. Nervously, he stared for a moment. Someone's face popped up and seemed to stare back. Tijas bolted.

Zelma laughed. "It's not *that* ancient, this technology," she said. It's opaque on the outside. Polarized! They can't see you."

Tijas saw them both laughing at him and he too laughed, though he couldn't cover up the ache he felt underneath it all.

***

Huge as a city, the delphinoid starship gradually became visible above the fused cities of Alykh and Shirénzang. It w.as night but the ship blotted out all the moons and most of the stars, a cetacean hole in the sky.

"Ah, Mikkálu-without-a-clan," Kyar Gharém said, as the walls of the chamber deopaqued. "I wish you could see what the people of your world are seeing. The dread! The terror! I know. I've been there."

The boy didn't seem quite as perky as before. Good. A dose of spectacle might temper his impertinence a bit.

"Magnify!" commanded Gharém, and the thinkhive complied, so that it seemed they were plunging headlong onto the surface.

"Boy! What are these places called?"

Spindly, crystalline, the flower petals smashed, peering from a wilderness of twisted metal —

"Nevéqilas — the Princely Palace!" said the childsoldier. "It's still there ... though the stem is bent."

"And there?"

Over a dark lake danced a thousand firebirds, each point of light reflected in the black still water —

"The Lake of Luminous Loons!" said the boy. "And the park is still there ... although ..."

Crawling across the park, a serpentine bridge of white metal.

"Magnify!"

The bridge — clearly not of a piece with the world called Urna. Seen close, the metal was etched with abstract shapes that vaguely suggested erotic couplings. It was an artifact of a pleasure world and did not blend with the natural colours of Urna which was no longer Urna.

On the bridge stood people. Staring up at the sky. Pointing. Wide-eyed. Different somatypes, different clothing; the folk of Urna a little more sallow, free-flowing robes in earth tones, the people of Alykh, in brash outfits, outrageous wigs and painted faces, yet all equally filled with fear.

"Already advance parties are marching through the city, announcing our intentions," Gharém said. "You were never collected in this way, I know — you were a single pickup. You missed one of the greatest spectacles that a shortliver can witness — a majestic display of the power of the High Inquest. Yes!" he went on, warming to his narrative, enjoying the childsoldier's discomfiture. "Landing parties parading through the streets, warning of the coming of ... *myself!* Kyar Gharém, most cunning of child collectors, he who lists are the most complete of any in the Dispersal!

"And soon they will come pouring forth — most willingly, but some to be ferreted out by finding birds, each bird imprinted with the DNA of its quarry — swooping and tearing through the squares and the strees — and I shall collect them all.

"At length, when the collection is done, a tachyon bubble will descend and I shall present the completed collection to my master, Hokh'Ton Ton Alkamathdes, who is called Supreme Hunter of Utopias. He will take from me the master list and another grand mission of mine shall be completed."

"It's sounds very ... impressive, my Lord, and yet —"

"What, child?" The childsoldier seemed meek after Gharém's little lecture. Perhaps he simply needed to pee. Servants should always be a little cowed, Gharém thought.

"Might it be possible for me to ... visit the home I grew up in?"

"You dare to ask me to divert the resources of this mission just so you can fraternize with whores?"

"My Lord, I just thought —"

Gharém did his most intimidating cackle, and was gratified to see the equerry droop once more. "You're in luck," he said. "At the start every momentous mission, I become rather ... sexually restless. I need — something to relax me a little. Or far too many will feel my wrath, and the High Inquest will rebuke me for doing my job with a little too much enthusiasm. So. I shall need the services of a decent servocorpse, and you, my child, shall guide me to the very best this broken down planet has to offer — for that, Mikkálu-without-a-Clan, is the only reason I picked you as my equerry."

Not to mention the fact that the boy had arrived at Bellares by special transport with a letter from the ruler of the world — the old world — a Princeling, and had not been genetically pre-chosen to be a childsoldier; this made the boy an enigma, a challenge, something to be deconstructed — dominated, if time permitted.

***

Forced to remain in the *zul*-cellar, living with the ache in the pit of his stomach that was his longing for his other self, Tijas dreamt of other worlds, of the overcosm that cannot be described except as a means to madness.

Far from the tutelage of Arbát, the words of the sung he had begun to sing returned unbidden:

in dárein shirenzheh

the silence between the stars ...

Tijas thought of the great gulf of nothingness separating star from star.

He thought of the light-mad overcosm, a legendary place where time and space where meaningless ... the ocean that the delphinoids sailed ... and he wondered if he would ever see it, if he would be driven mad, as many claimed ... and these words came to him:

den om verék en-tinjet
in-dárein shirenzheh ...

No living man has touched
the silence between the stars....

Eleven

Tunnels and Floaters

Arrogant, capricious, smug. That's who my Lord *Gharém is,* Mikkálu thought as the hoverfloat descended to Urna. *But it's a little more cushy than the war on Kishwá.*

In fact, the High Lord had been easy to manipulate. Mikkálu had grown up in a Temple of Aërat. He knew a little about seduction, which is not much about giving, and a lot about holding back; not much revealing, and a great deal of hinting. Mikkálu had figured out very quickly that Gharém's greatest fetish was to dominate, but one had to be a bit out of line to make the act of oppression satisfying to the oppressor. He figured out, too, that Gharém had a crippling terror of the Inquestors, yet yearned to ape their power.

A childsoldier seems easy enough to dominate; he is after all a child. But every childsoldier carries death in his eyes. Without the conditioning of absolute and unquestioning compliance to every command of the High Inquestors, an army of childsoldiers who would be chaos a thousandfold.

And anyone placed in command of a childsoldier, who was not an Inquestor, also lived with a subliminal dread.

Mikkálu had learned much in a very short time. *I'm a survivor,* he would tell himself, always.

He had been touting the skills of the servocorpses of Aërat since they left Bellares. To lead Gharém to the temple would mean he would get to see Éluma.

But would she see him?

How much of a chasm between them had time dilation made? He was only a few months older. Was she an old woman?

He did not care. He loved her. He had even been curt to the Starry Highness to protect her.

These thoughts coursed through his mind as he waited on his mercurial master.

The floater descended.

Masked from outside view by a light bender, they fell through clouds and skirted a flock of loons, pinwheeling lights over the lake.

"Tell the floater where to go," Gharém said.

"It's difficult to say. There should be a square by the lake, a marketplace ... but instead there are all these haphazard buildings."

"Alykh did not have the advantage of princely designer," Gharém said. "Just navigate by feel." Mikkálu subvocalized some commands so that the floater skirted what was once the edge of Shirénzang. Now there were citizens of Urna living in makeshift dwellings made from crates and packing material and wandering around. The floater moved slowly over their heads, silent, unseen. Here an old woman cooking over a fire. A boy trying to stir an old thinkhive to life. Servocorpses walking in circles, their programming aborted. Walking for ever, as their energy supplies could be replenished by sunlight.

"There's a square I recognize, and the displacement plates look active," Mikkálu said, because he saw occasional people popping in and out of thin air. "We came here in the old days, to buy illicit dreamstuff."

He brought the floater, its inhabitants still hidden from view by a refraction shield, to a gentle landing against broken flagstones.

"This way, my Lord," he said, taking the shockingly familiar step of grabbing hold of Kyar Gharém's hand. "Soon you'll be playing at your darkest fantasies —"

"Impertinence!" said Gharém, and slapped the boy's face.

Mikkálu could of course have lasered off the Child Collector's hand with a eyeblink, but he held himself back. *A childsoldier is obedient.*

***

Sajit waited for his father. *At some point, he'll come. And he'll have to understand.*

He waited, while Éluma attended to a ritual of the goddess. For the temple had not lost its appeal or its devotees; rather, being appended to what was now a pleasure city had increased the number of suppliants. It was exotic. It reeked of an ancient time.

Finally, Orifec came. Tired. World-weary, indeed. *I'll just tell him quickly. I'll be gone before he's thought about it.*

"Father, I am going. I've waited long enough."

"That's insane. You know what is about to happen."

"I talked to Éluma but she can never understand. She doesn't know about Tijas."

"And she cannot know."

"Tijas ... he's this *thing* gnawing inside of me. I'm not complete without him. And there's music. I'm not learning anything. Tijas is out there somewhere. I know it."

"Perhaps he's already been taken."

"Father, you're ... *callous*. You are a doppling. You understand."

"And you're my son. Who I gave up for his own protection, and who I'll never give up again."

"You could have kept me."

"Sajitteh...."

"Why couldn't I have grown up in the whorehouse, with my real mother?"

"I've told you. You have a destiny. You're going to be a great artist. I couldn't keep you close to me, stifling your dreams, imprisoned by privilege."

"You could have kept me!" Sajit screamed. "You engineered all this because you want to live your stupid dreams of being a musician through me ... but you'll never be me." Sajit started pummeling Orifec with his fists, hitting out wildly, even yanking out a hank of his hair.

Orifec couldn't stop himself. He clouted his son hard on the shoulder. Sajit became subdued. He was crying. "You hurt me," he said. "Tijas would never hurt me." Which he knew to me untrue. Because the emptiness in his stomach that was Tijas' absence was worse than being hit. Orifec looked at his hand. He was trembling.

"I can't believe I struck you," he said softly. Then his face became set and grim. Sajit had never seen Orifec this way. His shoulder stung; Orifec had clearly not struck many people, did not know his own strength. He was confused, unsettled.

Orifec grabbed Sajit by the shoulders. "Understand, Sajitteh," he said. "I'm doing this because I love you."

He pushed Sajit into a corridor, turned a corner, stepped on a displacement plate, and they found themselves in a strange bare room, with harsh, right-angled corners.

"I'm going to keep you here," Orifec said, "and I'm going to key the displacement field to my DNA only. I'll bring you some food and you can relieve yourself in that sanitizer," he pointed to an elimination stool in the corner. "You'll stay here until they're gone."

"Tijas!"

"We created him to take your place, Sajit. That is why we broke the law and tradition and made that abomination. You know that in Urna, a doppling cannot live."

"Except you, you hypocrite," Sajit whispered harshly.

His father did not reply.

"I've spoken to people from other worlds. On some planets, dopplings are called twins, and they are treated with honour, they're even considered lucky in some places. The abomination thing is just ignorance — because we're a backworld — a planet that hasn't evolved."

"I can't listen to this," Orifec said. And vanished from the box of a room.

***

"Wake up, Tijas!" Daro said. "We're leaving the planet."

The troupe was gathered in the *zul* cellar. Tijas struggled to open eyes and he could see them all, shadows in the ill-lit room.

"You don't need to leave," Tijas said. "You've just started a good operation. The place'll be swarming with *dorezdas* soon. You'll be rich, you'll be able to get a real place, open a theater."

He waited. No one answered, but he became aware that the whole team was looking at him. "Not because of me?"

"Tisseh," said the Professor, and Tijas realized it was the first time anyone had called him by his child-name. Even Sajit had never done so.

"We're a team, Tijas. We're a family. We want you to come with us."

"Sajit, too?"

"Yes," Daro said, "if we can find him."

Tijas's mind raced. *If we can find him* ... how?

"You think I've been doing nothing, puttering upstairs with the thinkhive of this building?" said Zelma. "I've been planning an escape."

"There's a network of interconnected tunnels" she went on, fluttering her rainbow lashes, "and deep in the bowels of this building, there's a displacement nexus. I can divert power, reprogram it to magnify its range a millionfold, send us to a spot on one of the moons ... just outside the Inquestral perimeter."

"Think of it, Tijas," Daro said. "Freedom. No more living in the shadows. We'll ride the space between spaces, go from world to world and play out our timeless dramas in city squares in each world we come to."

"Yes, take us where dopplings are not *harám*," said Tijas, "where we can go about in the streets and not be seen as abominations."

"That's right," Daro said. *He doesn't seem that convinced*, Tijas thought.

"When can I go and fetch Sajit?"

"Well ..."

"You said he could come with us."

"If we can find him," Daro said.

"I *can* find him," said Tijas. "I've got a compass in my mind that leads to him, and that's how I know he's alive ... alive and scared."

For when he closed his eyes, he saw a room. A
room, peculiarly square, not pleasingly rounded like a
normal human dwelling. A prison. And felt pain.
Sharp pain in the shoulder, as if he had been beaten.
Could feel hot tears on his own cheeks, though his eyes
were dry.

"I know *exactly* where he is. I feel it."

"You feel *something*," Zelma said. "But is it Sajit, or
is your own sense of loss?"

Tijas reached deep into the source of his pain.

*Could I have made up this pain, to compensate
myself for emptiness, because to feel pain is still better
than to feel nothing at all?*

Tijas felt doubt, and in that moment he felt weak;
he knew that Daro and Zelma loved him, and that this
entire foolhardy plan had been cooked up for *his*
benefit, that all of them in their minds had already
given Sajit up to the brutal machinery of the High
Inquest.

I'm the only one who thinks he can be rescued, he
thought. Maybe I've already lost this battle.

In that moment he said, "Maybe I'll come. Maybe I
will."

***

The Child Collector and the equerry stepped from
plate to plate, Gharém barely catching up as the boy
lightly skipped the distance between displacements.
As they reached the pathway leading to the entrance to
the Temple of Aërat, Mikkálu saw his master grow
grimmer, more brooding.

People like him are all the same, he thought.

This part of Shirenzang was still operational. Indeed, people in the brash clothing of Aírang were moving up the pathway — they had discovered something in this backward world congruent with their own world's preoccupations.

They were not dressed to be conspicuous. As they left the parked floater, Gharém had made them don refracting robes. Even had they been noticed, they might not have been seen as two people, but as something else in the area — trees, or walls. They blended.

"I may be occupied for some time," said Gharém. "I'm going to give charge of some very important items." He handed Mikkálu a pouch. "Tuck that into your tunic and don't lose it."

"Ha! Am I holding your entire career in my hands, Lord Gharém?"

"Perhaps."

Mikkálu could imagine what was in the pouch. It was both soft like flesh and articulated, like a fine metal mesh. When he squeezed it, it squirmed.

"Use it well," Gharém said, "and help me carry out this operation as smoothly and efficiently as possible, to the greater glory of the High Compassion." And Gharém handed over a few other objects: a message disk linked to the delphinoid's shipboard thinkhive, an a credit plaque with the Inquestral sigil. "Don't spend it all on sweets," he said. "Now instruct the attendants in your brothel for me, as I am too exalted a figure to bargain with corpses."

"It's not a brothel, my lord, it's a temple."

"Semantics, boy."

At the gateway to the temple, the servocorpse appeared to take their requests. A sight he had known all through childhood, and a familiar servocorpse, stepping out of the shadows.

The collector seemed almost reticent, letting Mikkálu take the lead.

"Tork! Don't you recognize me?"

"It's been a few years. You are unchanged."

"And so are you. Because you're a corpse. You don't get to age."

"And you have been sailing the space between spaces, young master."

"Yes. I have a ... suppliant. He seeks something special. He is one of great importance. He carries the Inquestral aegis. He wishes to be loved by the dead."

"And the dead are at their most loving in this temple, for those who are able to afford it."

"Let's just say that my master's credit is at an Inquestral level."

"Then he shall have all he needs, including insurance against forfeiture for any love objects crippled or damaged by the encounters." The servocorpse appeared to roll his eyes; but Mikkálu knew they did not possess irony.

"I'm sure my master will appreciate being given full rein."

"Which of the disciplines of the art of love is he most interested in?"

The Child Collector interrupted. "Subjugation. Submission. Absolute Subservience."

"Nice boss," Tork said it so only Mikkálu could hear.

"I was just thinking that you don't understand irony."

"I've been reprogrammed since you were last here," said the dead man. "The people of Alykh have different tastes. They don't take religion that seriously, and they prefer it when a corpse acts fresh."

Irony? This time the corpse betrayed nothing of the kind.

"Powers of powers, Tork," Mikkálu whispered, "take him to your grandest coupling chamber and give him all he wants."

The servocorpse bowed almost in two (servocorpses not being constrained by pain, such contortions were de rigeur) and said, "Your Lordship shall have paradise, though but for a spell."

"It is not paradise I require," said Gharém, "but the depths of darkness. And it shall not be for a spell, but for at least two sleeps. I shall create, oh, such a hell, I shall thrive on fear."

"What is a hell, my Lord?" said the servocorpse.

"It's something religious," Mikkálu said. "Quick, take him. And tell me where to find who I've come to see."

"After ten years, you demand to see *her?*" said the corpse. "Do you realize who she is now? Do you have an appointment?"

***

"Have I failed?" Orifec cried out. "Éllekeh, I was about to beat him! And now I've locked him up. I didn't listen to him."

In an inner room somehow connecting the palace

and the temple — though not directly, for the path between them was a mishmash of displacement plates that crisscrossed the city — they clung together, the dispossessed princeling and the obsolescent goddess.

"They're resilient. You should know. I know. We both were raised in difficult environments, by people with other priorities," Éluma said. "Go talk to him again."

He didn't answer.

"There's something you're not telling me," she said. "I suppose it's some kind of father-son secret. Whatever it is, it can't be the end of the world."

He smiled wryly. "I suppose not. After all, the world has already ended."

They lay together on a cushion of force, slung between pillars made in the shape of the royal insignia; the twisted serpent columns had been rescued from the old audience chamber.

"Let's go and see him," she said.

"I'm afraid to."

"You are a Starry Highness. Don't let a child bully you."

"I understand that children can have an infinite capacity to forgive their parents," she said.

"But you don't know that. I don't know that. We haven't really had parents," said Orifec.

"We'll take him some food," she said.

"Let me get dressed."

Orifec picked up a piece of clingfire and wrapped it about his loins, then threw on an overshirt. Éluma looked at him. "You're dressing up to speak to your own child?"

He said, "It's almost an audition."

At that moment, they heard the voice of the thinkhive.

There is a petition for the goddess herself, it said.

Éluma laughed. "You know I don't take petitions in person anymore," he said. "Silly thinkhive."

No, this is a petition that you must honour. It comes with an Inquestral sigil.

"An Inquestor seeks the attentions of a goddess?" said Orifec. "That, you'll have to honor."

***

Stairwells — the ancient kind — round and round, descending into darkness.   Circling down stairwells that sometimes veered and twisted.   A claustrophobic burrow, musty air.

Everything had been left behind.   No changes of clothing. No souvenirs. Whether from Urna or Alykh, the past would be obliterated.

Now a passageway where even Tijas had to bend. And where they emerged was a circular room with a circular displacement plate, wide enough for a dozen people or a load of cargo.

The room was illumined by a pale blue sourceless light.   Its walls were blank, metallic, but there was an exposed panel from which trailed tendrils of metal and fibrillating neuron strands, with triangular light-shapes.

They squeezed against the walls, making sure they did not step on the plate before Zelma instructed them to.   The magician was hunched over some light dice, making them circle and fly.   The acrobats looked nervous, in the cramped space.

Zelma said, "I've almost finished the reprogramming." She moved her hands over the patches of light, and the triangles blinked and changed color, gold, silver, pink; the neuron strands, woven from the tissue of recycled servocorpses, swayed, separated, reconnected.

As he watched her, the pain in the pit of Tijas' stomach grew stronger.

Sajit is in a room like this room.

"The delphinoid and its accompanying craft have established a perimeter within the orbit of Urna's first moon," Zelma said. "But on the third moon, there's a little backworld starport. We should be able to hitch a ride somewhere. All we have to do is put on a play there — move people. Engage their passions. In this galaxy, singers of songs and those who tell stories always have free passage."

"The offers'll come rolling in," Daro said.

Sajit can't get out! And he's calling to me!

"Are you all right, Tijas?" the magician asked.

"Yes." But he wasn't.

"The space between spaces!" said one of the acrobats. "The feeling! You can't explain it!"

"Of course not," said the other acrobat. "They put you in stasis for the whole flight."

Daro said, "Those two haven't actually done star travel — unless you count being stuffed into a people bin."

"It's done!" said the Professor. The room hummed and the walls sparkled.

The ache grew stronger.

"Listen carefully. You must subvocalize the correct command, and the window will be open only for a few minutes. And here are the syllables. You must subvocalize them exactly, or it will not work. All together ... *kha-na-ta-shé-vis.*"

She had barely said it when the musician was already wavering — a trick of the light? No. This amplified displacement was pulling a lot of power, was not instantaneous. He grew faint, became an outline of shimmering blue, then seemingly collapsed into a point and vanished.

The others were starting to vanish now.

"Quick, Tisseh! The window is closing!" Zelma said, but then she vanished.

The pain was unbearable. The emptiness that needed to be filled with his doppling, calling out to him, demanding that he enter —

He concentrated all his thoughts on the subvocalization ... *kha-na-ta-SAJIT!*

No!

He looked around him. All his new friends were shimmering, popping out. He looked at his hands, solid flesh — *I've failed!* — he thought, his hands shaking but still solid. *Sajit! Sajit!* he cried out with his mind. Tried to focus on the room, the darkness, the captivity of his brother. *Take me to Sajit!*

And then, looking down at his hands, he saw they were no longer there. And the *nothingness* was creeping up his arms. His feet were disappearing. The *nothingness* was crawling up his legs.

"Sajit!" he screamed.

Twelve
Loving the Dead

Kyar Gharém was led by two torchbearing dead children through a down-sloping passageway to a cave. — whether natural or made by art he could not tell. The air was cold; his breath hung in the dimness.

He was dressed in a fanciful costume belonging to no world that anyone knew of; there were leather leggings, a swirling cloak of black fire, and chains of some strange alloy that was oxidising in the moistness of the chamber; there was artificial shimmerfur, out of deference to the Inquestors, but his fantasy was more ancient than the Dispersal of Man — he had discovered it in a history of Old Earth, and it had ever lodged itself in his mind.

It was from this myth that much of the terminology of the Inquestors came, mused the author of this quasi-history. They were called Inquisitors, and they were given free rein to torture as they pleased, the better to purify the souls of those they ruled, and to cleanse their hearts of the condition of being fallen beings.

And doubtless, they found torture to be quite fetishizing. As did Gharém. And to be indulged only at these moments. Breathing in the foul air of the simulated dungeon, he was already becoming quite excited.

Gharém had ancient instruments to hand; meathooks, nail-rippers, tongue extractors, iron maidens. Now it was time to consummate his fantasy.

"Confess!" he cried out.

Around him, bodies began to stir. They began to draw breath. They were everywhere. A woman with exaggerated curves, her breasts straining against a membraneous slip. A dwarf with a monstrous penis that trailed the ground. Children and old women with slithering, clattering tongues. Oiled gladiators, chained against crumbling columns. As his eyes grew used to the darkness he saw a row of people of all colors and sexes, impaled against the wall, moaning and thrusting, for the stakes they were impaled on were gigantic and phallic and alive.

And they moaned, *Master ... master ...*

They had outdone themselves!

Gharém selected a lead-tipped flagellum from the array of instruments and began swinging it. The servocorpses writhed.

"Confess your heresies," he rasped, "and then be liberated as I rape all of you to death."

He cracked the flagellum. The servocorpses writhed.

They were all already dead anyway. Let them die again. And again. They were his, there only to do his bidding, and to be crushed regardless of how well they obeyed.

***

Éluma decided to meet this carrier of the Inquestral sigil in the Chamber of the Goddess. This was not a place of gold and statues and dancing lights, but a severe room, pyramidal in shape, lit by a single flaming crystal. She decided that she would greet him clothed only in light.

Her mind was in turmoil, with thoughts of Orifec and the confusion of dealing with her son. But she had never served an Inquestor. That would have to be the pinnacle of one's vocation.

So she adjusted the clouds to be at their most cushiony, to flow around her person in both a comforting and a seductive manner, and waited.

Presently, the thinkhive spoke.

Goddess, it said, *the bearer of the Inquestral sigil is approaching.*

She stood before the fire-crystal, closed her eyes, and stretched her arms out over the flames.

Two small hands grasped hers. A child's hands.

The opened her eyes.

The boy laughed....

The boy who smiled in the shadows, so many years ago —

"Mikeh!" she laughed out laughed and embraced him. "But — how?"

"I carry the sigil of the High Inquest," the boy said. "I'm not supposed to use it this way, but it's the only way they'd let me see you."

She remembered —

The laser-eyes, the citrine fire shooting from them, slicing and cauterizing a woman's hand —

"Mikeh!" she said. "Years have gone by."

"For me, it was only a month."

"Even so ... you didn't come here for sex." If he was only a month older — although in *her* time, so much had transpired —

Mikkálu laughed. "I'm getting older," he said. "And ... I've *seen* things. I grew up here."

"You are *one month* older, little boy, and I'm *not* scared of you, even if you *could* slice me in to with a glance."

"It's fine. I'm not in battle mode."

"And now I'm old enough to be your mother, and I *am* a mother, too. Oh — Mikeh — you have to help us!"

And Mikkálu said, "Yes, Ellekeh, that's why I've come."

And she understood that his coming was no accident. It was *meúr*.

***

Gharém roared! The whip raised welts on dead flesh. Rivers of haemosimulant fountained and flowed. Naked corpses writhed and thrust against their chains.

A dark, tall servocorpse with many breasts and filed teeth gnawed at his gnarled manhood. Gharém yanked out hanks of dead hair, shrieking in an ecstasy that was pain's mirror-doppling.

At that moment, a message disk blinked.

He grunted, extracted his penis from the perilous orifice, and turned to look at it.

Delphinoid secure field in place, Lord Collector. Finding birds primed and programmed. Thinkhives ready. Containment field floaters, long-range displacement devices activated. Preliminary surveys done and collection should net close to 100%. We await your signal, Lord Collector.

But the dead were dancing ...

"I'll give the signal," said Gharém, "as soon as I complete my exercise regimen."

Dead men, women, and children screamed in simulated pain. "I am your ruler!" Gharém cried. "Your owner! Your master! Confess your sins!"

***

Alone in the prison, Sajit thought only of his doppling. His doppling consumed everything. In the gloom, he smelled his own hands, sniffed at his elbows, his armpits, knowing it was his doppling's scent.

How could the Starry Highness have done this to his own flesh and blood? Sajit was shaking.

The gloom deepened and he felt as though he was careening into an abyss —

Yet the feeling of Tijas' presence kept intensifying. He was so close! The scent of Tijas wasn't just his own scent. There was something else in the air. The air was growing thicker — more solid — a shape wavering in the emptiness —

If he reached out to hug the darkness, he could almost —

And suddenly, Tijas was hugging him for real. He had materialized on the displacement plate. The *locked* displacement plate.

"I'm going —"

"Crazy, no you're not, I —"

"Yes, crazy, this yawning emptiness, only —"

"You understand —"

— *Enough of finishing each other's sentences,* Sajit thought.

And Tijas heard!

— *We don't have to talk anymore.*

— *This apartness — it's strengthened the way we can reach other — I can hear you —*

— *In my head, louder than —*

— *Ever before —*

"Stop," said Sajit. "It's too —"

"Overwhelming. I know."

Sajit and Tijas sat for a moment. The tips of their fingers touched. There was an electricity there. Sajit could hear the thoughts, pounding at him from every side, but he realized he could turn them down, if he concentrated.

"We have to ... talk to each other normally," Tijas said. "We are freaks as it is. Have you been in here long? I felt it ... so powerfully ... a day ago."

"Daro? The Professor?"

"They went off-world. They did it to save me. Us, really, but they all thought you'd been captured already. They couldn't —"

"Feel me, like we can."

"Orifec has done this to protect you," Tijas said. "He doesn't understand."

"We can't let anyone see us!"

"They've got these birds. *Finding birds,* they call them. They're like birds of prey, each one locked on a single target."

"But there's two of us. We can confuse it."

"How can we get away?"

"I don't know. The displacement plate is locked. Orifec keyed it to his DNA."

"Isn't there something here we can use? An old article of clothing, a bloodstain?"

"No. This isn't a room he normally uses ... wait." Sajit reached inside the pocket of his tunic. Was it still there? "I fought him really hard. I think I pulled out some of his hair."

Triumphant, he found the handful of hair and showed it to his doppling.

"Maybe if we sprinkle it in the center of displacement plate —"

"But what command can we give it? I don't know where to go, I don't even really know where I am, or how exactly I got here, except somehow your voice inside my head was so strong it overrode a thinkhive that the Professor had personally hacked and jimmied and reprogrammed to send us to a moon —"

Sajit said, "Hold still. Together, we'll focus on a safe place."

Sajit and Tijas sat facing each other on the displacement plate, then Sajit took the hank of the Princeling's hair and place the strands carefully around them, encircling the two boys. "Closer," Sajit said. They squeezed together, locking legs and arms to take up as little room as they could.

They would have to stay inside the thin line.

They knew no special subvocalizations. They would have to focus on one thing: *safety, safety,* hoping the thinkhive would be programmed to —

Sajit saw his brother's shape start to shimmer a little. It wasn't working right! "Hold tight!" he said, thinking at least if they were going to become a cloud of particles somewhere in space, they would at least be together....

Another figure began to form in the same space as theirs — an unthinkable anomaly — they would be destroyed for sure! — and Sajit looked up, hugging his doppling even harder to himself, and saw —

Orifec! Glowering, looking down at the boys who were occupying his space, and his mouth was opening, he was about to speak when —

The room vanished and they were still alive, still together — but what was the place that the thinkhive had designated as *safety?*

***

Éluma deopaqued the Chamber of the Goddess and led Mikkálu through a small portal that displaced to her private quarters, and she found Orifec with his head buried in his hands.

"What happened?" she said.

He said, "He's gone."

"Gone? From a locked room?"

"A locked, sealed, keyed-to-my-DNA room."

"Who could have have done this to us?" She sat beside him, looked at his face, and once again felt that he was hiding something. "There's something else. You have to tell me. What have you done with him?"

Orifec said, "I can't speak of it!"

Mikkálu had followed her in. He spoke up now. "Starry Highness," he said.

"You!" Orifec said furiously.

"Don't!" she said. "He hasn't done anything."

Éluma saw that boy felt awkward, intruding on his Princeling's grief.

"Mikeh came to see us. He's working for —"

"The Child Collector," Mikkálu said. "He brought me along as his equerry. Well, personal slave, really. He doesn't like to use servocorpses, likes the power of actually intimidating a living person — especially one who could decapitate him with a glance," he added, laughing.

"You haven't changed," Orifec said.

"It's only been a month for him," said Éluma. "Even so —"

"I've squirmed out of a year's worth of trouble," Mikkálu said. "Got out of a lot of boring training by flattering the commanders and their lieutenants. Caught a big one — His Arrogant Lordship, Kyar Gharém, Collector to the High Inquest."

Even Orifec smiled a little.

"But I've come to see you in a time of turmoil," Mikkálu said. "Can I help?"

"How could you help?" Éluma said. "You, a child still."

"A deadly child," Mikkálu said. "But I *can* help."

"Yes, you can," Orifec said bitterly. "Persuade the Collector to go home. This collection should be aborted anyway, considering that the High Inquest has muddled its *makrúgh* and mixed up two different games. And destroyed millions of lives."

"In the High Compassion," Mikkálu whispered by habit. The ritual formula rang hollow. "Starry Highness, you know I can't do that. But I can find your son. I'm the only person who can."

***

— whirling, a kaleidscoping whirlwind of thoughts, blending, meshing, interconnecting —

Tijas! Where are you?

I'm inside you! *Inside-outside-around-among-within-surrounding-melding* —

A space. A space without dimensions. A time outside time.

The space resolved, it seemed, into a room of sorts. It couldn't be a real room because it had no walls. It had no up and down. And Sajit felt himself resolving. He felt the part of himself that he could feel as *I* pull reluctantly from the blended vortex.

We're in the space between spaces, he said without speaking. Without, if one can imagine it, even thinking.

We're in the place we always go to, in the femtosecond between displacements, Tijas said, *but the place we go to is too brief to have meaning. No human being could ever perceive this.*

Indeed, how could it be perceived when the snippet of spacetime one travelled through was too brief to transgress the limits of uncertainty?

It must be because we travelled together, Sajit said, *entwined, and with DNA that cannot be untangled —*

— and because we did not give a clear command to pin down coordinates.

The thinkhive that managed displacements was being forced to delve into its memories to piece together a credible set of coordinates. Perhaps it was examining all the places this DNA had been before, in the short time it had been alive ... and sometimes in more than one place at the same time. It was taking long enough in its calculations for a perceptible moment to be generated. It was in this tiny moment that the two were able to communicate.

It's amazing — I'm inside of you, everywhere inside of you —

I think this is what adults are feeling when they talking about "bursting their milkpods" —

Laughter, cascading like a meteor shower!

I want this moment to last forever —

Yes! Forever and ever!

But it was already over.

They were in a forest.

In a chill gray space.

A pool of light in a deep dark forest.

Sajit spoke first, with words, because even the thoughts that passed freely between them were nothing compared to the intimacy they had shared in the space between spaces.

"So this is how the planetary thinkhive parsed the word *safety,*" he said.

Tijas said, "I've never been here, but I know it well."

"Walk a little further in, and we'll come to a wall. And the ruins of a temple. And in that direction ... my old house."

"We have to be very quiet," Tijas. "The moons will be singing soon."

In a few minutes they had reached the clearing that Sajit knew so well. The moons were rising all at once. Eríkion tumbled in a skein of cloud. Half-Káruval glowered behind full Arrisát. Kalíth and Ralíth circled each other, and the scent of *vanjéris* laced the air. Soon the rosella petals would start to fall, moonlit dust-motes in the deep night.

And in a few minutes the moons sang. Oh, Sajit knew now that they did not sing, that the music was the song his heart heard, woven from loneliness and silence.

Above the wuthering and the sighing in the trees, the voices of the moons were his own voice. But so clear ...

Den táthes eyáh —
Den Sirana

but this was no inner voice. Sajit turned and saw that it was Tijas who was singing. It was as though he was watching himself, in that lost world, when Urna was Urna, and a song was just a song.

"You've seen this place," Sajit said.

"Yes. I've seen everything now. When we were in the space between spaces, and we were both everywhere and nowhere."

Tijas took Sajit's hand. With complete familiarity, sure of every step, every old stone and every tree trunk. "There's a temple ... a little further."

Sajit said, "Even I never went there. It is too far from home."

"Let's go there. Everything's too far from home now. Home doesn't exist."

Tijas found the displacement plate, buried under leaves. Hand in hand the hopped onto it and reemerged in another clearing. Sajit had hoped for another time-stretched moment of melding, but the displacement was barely a blink.

The temple had an entrance, but no roof save for a canopy intertwined branches. Here the trees were generations old and had linked to form a leafy roof, replacing the old dead plastiforms. A holosculpt stood, its arms long broken off, half-buried in a profusion of weeds. It was of stone, and its face was the face of Éluma. Centuries old, but still the face of the love-goddess.

"My mother," Sajit.

"But not mine," said Tijas.

"I want us to merge, like we did in the space between spaces."

"We can't."

"Then, the way grownups do." Sajit said, "I've been in the Temple of Aërat, Tijas. I've seen what they do. What Arbát wanted from us. What the suppliants get from the servocorpses."

Impulsively, he kissed his doppling. Not as a brother, but as he'd seen in darkened corners of the temple. Startled, Tijas pulled away. "Weird," he said, wiping his mouth. "What happens next?"

"I think we're supposed to take our clothes off."

"Why? It's chilly."

"I think we're supposed to try to meld. Not with our minds but with our ... our *selves.*"

"It sounds stupid," Tijas said, but he had already shed his tunic. Through gaps in the leaves above, a hundred little shafts of light pierced his slim body. *I'm looking at myself,* Sajit thought. He too stepped out of his thin clingfire. "So we just look at each other?" Tijas said.

"I don't know, but somehow, after a lot of grunting, it leads to the bursting of milkpods," Sajit said.

They both started laughing, then, and presently they fell asleep in the moonlight, on the bed of weeds beneath the statue of the goddess Aërat, who was also Sajit's human mother, with their garments heaped up and tangled over their intertwined limbs. And the moons sang a lullaby.

Sajit dreamed of a time when Tijas was not. Of his sisters, his parents, his village home. Of standing alone in the clearing. Presently, he came awake; of all the moons, only Eríkion was left, circling above the treetops, shifting the dappling patterns on his doppling's pale skin.

His memories of the time before Tijas were gauzelike, faded. *Before he came,* he thought, *I wasn't really me yet.*

Mulling over this paradox, he slid back into sleep.
***

In another temple, almost as ancient, Kyar Gharém was the principal in a ritual far less innocent. He was coming to climax, wading through a sea of blood and entrails. He kissed a corpulent corpse, biting and ripping out her tongue. A dead woman wrapped an extruded intestine about his loins. He was in an ecstasy of torment.

He never wanted it to end.

He was drunk on his savage appetites. Again and again he plunged into writhing flesh. Death-rattles came again and again, for the dead may rattle more than once.

Once more he climaxed in a torrent of blood.

He lay on a bed of corpses, heaving. Incongruously, a neatly dressed page brought in a beaker of fresh *zúl* on an iridium platter. The walls dissolved and the programming was replaced by a rustic scene of meadows and rosella groves.

The page was not dead; his class of clientele merited some living servitors. If he *was* a corpse, it must be a very fine model indeed.

"Is your name Mikkálu?" Gharém asked.

"No, my lord. Though many of us *are* named that. There was a Mikkálu here once who made a name for himself, ten years ago ... many of us took his name because of that. He became a childsoldier ... by choice. Everyone knows the story of how he defied the law — and how the Starry Highness changed the law for love of the goddess."

"And are you not afraid of the coming of the Child Collector?"

"If I am on the list," the boy said, "it is *meúr*. No one can resist."

"Such enchanting superstitions you people have! I could tell you that answer," Gharém said, "with a flick of my mind."

"If it *is* to be *meúr*," the boy said, "I'd be happier not knowing in advance."

"You wouldn't want to seduce me into granting a reprieve?"

"What good would it do? Everything in this temple is at your disposal, my lord. Should you wish to sate your pleasure on my person, the goddess would demand my compliance."

"You are not to my taste. Just go instruct your whoremaster to run this scenario one more time. The task I am about to do is not entirely to my liking ... I would rather experience the love of the dead ... for they have no free will."

Gharém could not help noticing that the page sauntered off with a smirk. An inferior who could be crushed with a word, but he looked down on Gharém's dark fantasies.

Let them despise me! he thought. *It comes with the job. On any planet where a Child Collector has landed, he is always the most hated person in the world.*

***

Orifec did not know how this childsoldier could find his sons, let alone save them. He knew only that once, before Sajit was even born, this boy had boldly burst in among the acolytes and saved Éluma. There was something more than bluster in him.

"I need to be up high," Mikkálu said. "As high above the city as possible."

"Come, then," Orifec said. "Shirénzang's elevators are not all broken." For he still knew how to find what remained of his old palace.

The Princeling led them through a corkscrew hallway to a displacement shaft. Mikkálu gasped as the circle they stood on hurtled skyward, the varigravs not quite in alignment so it was not a smooth, quiet ride but a rattling, stomach-turning journey through a crystal tunnel which was now bent in places.

At times they stopped to navigate a corridor on foot. Orifec moved purposefully; he had made this journey a few times since the people bins had landed. When Éluma had been busy with the business of the goddess, he had wandered these clear tubular pathways that had once formed the elegant stem and stamens of the flower-palace. There had been the remnants of a planetary council; though his world was reduced to a square inside a new metropolis, yet it still counted as its own world with this own culture, its own governance.

Éluma gripped his hand. They did not speak.

Many petals of the crystal flower that formed the palace that once overlooked the city had been sheared off, and the topmost turret was broken and doubled downward against the stem. Orifec found the passageway he was looking for, leaning precariously over a wall of glass and emptying out into his former throneroom. He eased himself down and helped Éluma.

Mikkálu leaped onto the throneroom. The columns of intertwining servocorpose pythonoids still stood. There was a throne, too, though it had been open to the elements, and — in a most unroyal fashion — was covered in bird droppings.

"We have two sleeps at most, probably only one," said Mikkálu, before the old lecher tires of his bloody fantasies. We will have to find him quickly."

Orifec said, "Are we high enough yet?"

The throneroom's walls were shattered. Here and there, forcefields were still in place; through gaps, a cold wind blasted them. Going to the very edge of the throneroom, which teetered as they walked across, the boy looked over the edge. Orifec said, "The parts of my world that are still standing ... a few temple, some deserted squares, beneath them all a network of tunnels that predates the displacement system ... over there, the bridge and the lake where the luminous loons gather. And sprouting from the wreckage, another planet ... bustling, mercantile, kaleidoscopic ... nothing like our simple world. It will soon swallow all that remains of Urna."

Over the lake, something ominous: a ship, as wide, it seemed, as the lake itself, blotting out an entire quadrant of the sky. The ship was ovoid and featureless.

There were none of the lights, fins, spirals and jags that a pleasure ship would have; it was plain and functional ... a ship for warriors. Its only surface feature was a silvery-black whirling nebula.

"That is the delphinoid that will take your son," Mikkálu said. "But we can get to him first."

The equerry took a message disk from his tunic and held it to his forehead, along it to interface with his thoughts.

"I'm getting us a finding bird," the boy said.

"You can't!" Orifec said.

"What's a finding bird?" asked Éluma.

"It's what will find him," said Mikkálu, "a devilishly clever thing, its sensors honed to a single DNA-signature. It can look around corners, through opaqued windows, below the ground and in the sky. It can outfly any floater, any speeder. One childsoldier,

one finding bird.   It's relentless.   It'll find your boy,
dead or alive."

"And bring him to the Inquest! We're trying to stop
that!" Éluma said.

"Look!" the boy said, pointing.

From the whirling nebula on the belly of the
starship, a single point of light was detaching itself,
then soaring up, a comet against the starship's shadow,
a streak more bright than daylight, hurting his eyes,
hurtling downward now, towards them as they stood
on the unsteady parapet.   The dot grew larger and
Orifec saw now that it swooped on silver wings.
Abruptly its shadow was overhead.   An aquiline beak
and broad wingspan, and a bloodcurdling shriek as it
touched down now on the parapet and Orifec saw the
talons, sharp and wide enough to skewer a human
child.   It shrieked again, a cry at once animal-like and
metallic.

"This finding bird has been programmed with your
boy's identity."

"— but it will bring him straight to the Inquestors!
—" Éluma said. "It's taking him straight to his death!"

Mikkálu closed his eyes and when he opened them
he had armed his irises.   His eyes turned citrine.   He
leaped up, whirled, shouted "Ishá ha!" the childsoldiers'
warcry and as he somersaulted twin rays of laser light
sliced through one of the serpent columns.   The
parapet shuddered.   The finding bird flapped its wings,
each flap a peal of thunder.

"Not at all," said the childsoldier.   "Once the bird
finds the boy, I will slice him to ribbons.   No bird, no
childsoldier."

"Thank you," Éluma said.

"Now, does this throneroom fly?" said the equerry.

"I'll tell it to follow the bird," said Orifec. He subvocalized a few commands and the floor began to hum.

Slowly, it uncoupled itself from its force-moorings and headed out. The finding bird flapped its wings again and hovered over their heads, its large compound eyes rotating.

"You'll save my son," Éluma said. "I know you will. I always thought somehow you would come back."

The throneroom lifted off now, thrumming, and Orifec threw a reflecting mask over them so they could not be seen.

His heart was heavy. Events were spiralling out of control ... and he had still not dared to tell the goddess that there were two sons to be saved, not one.

NEXT ISSUE
BOOK FOUR
(continues)

LOST TALES

Remembrances

Original intro from *Asimov's Magazine:*

Mr. Sucharitkul once described his Inquestor Series as an attempt to create a universe of "incredible beauty and brutality." Certainly it has plenty of both. But when it was compared to the late Cordwainer Smith's Instrumentality of Mankind Series, Mr. Sucharitkul remarked that there were some similarities in the two imaginary universes, "but his is more Oriental." We don't understand this, putting it as Auctorial Inscrutability.

In the huge chamber, dwarfed by their gilded hoverthrones, a boy and a girl sat quietly by themselves. The boy was utterly still, numbed. Beneath them, shrouded in shadow and ceremonial vestments, lay the corpse of their father.

The girl sprang from her throne. The boy did not move, but followed his sister with his eyes. She clapped her hands, dissolving the dark walls to reveal the dying city below. Tall walls crumbling into cindercrusts. Streams of liquid light that shattered the milky-glass clouds, so artfully crafted by a generation of cloud-sculptors — light that struck the twisted towers and the jewelled minarets and made them vanish in puffs of smoke. Fire chasing fire in the labyrinthine gardens.

There was no sound; the forceshields screened out the screams. But the boy could make out people at last, tiny dots of people . . . insects being flushed out of their nests. He forced himself to watch. Towers cracking open like ripe fruits, seed-pod-people tumbling, snapping into flame, sizzling, plummeting. . . .

Quietly, his sister was saying, "We should have gone out with the people bins. There was plenty of warning."

"Father's dead."

"If they find us here they'll separate us, assign us to different clans. The Inquest won't let us grow up together."

He leapt from his throne then, hugging the dead Princeling. The body was ice-cold, stone-hard. "I want to die," the boy said.

"Yes." Their eyes met over the body. Glint of a dagger drawn suddenly from the girl's kilt. The old traditional weapon of the city's ruling house. No painless euthanasia for a prince of the blood. He saw her smile sadly. We're only nine years old!, the boy was thinking. This can't really be happening to us. . . . They were matched twins, destined from birth to share throne and bed. For thousands of years the Inquest had not touched their world, had ruled it from afar . . . and now came war. What they fought over no one knew, but the planet's fate was sealed. In an orbit around one of the moons, people bins waited to collect the survivors, to time-freeze them in stasis until an unused world could be found for them; for the Inquest was compassionate, and avoided, if it could, the waste of human life.

"Quick, the dagger," he said. "Before we change our minds."

"No . . . one more look . . ." She rose and turned to the wallshields. Smoke blotted out the suns. And now, bursting through the darkstriped clouds, a tower-string of childsoldiers riding their mirror-flashing hoverdisks. Never breaking their formation, like links in a chain that hung from the sky. The children all whirling, whirling endlessly, twin lances of light bursting from their laser-irises, spinning disks of deadly light . . . buildings sawn instantly into toppling chunks! Sliced people tumbling into heaps on the streets! And the fire —

"They're coming closer! Let's get it over with!" the boy whispered, hoarse.

"But I must see this — I must never forget — "

"What for, sister? It's over. What do you mean, never forget? It's over!"

Then they hugged one another, not passionately but ceremonially, as kings do. He seized the knife from her. "I'll do it first."

The noise burst on them. The shields were broken. The knife slipped from his hands. Tendrils of smoke curled in through the dissipating shielding. And behind the smoke were dozens of the childsoldiers. They wore black war-tunics. Their eyes — their weapons — glittered crystal-gold. Their faces were hard, pitiless.

They were here. It was too late to observe tradition. "Why?" the girl was screaming. "Why did you come here? We had such a beautiful world, we harmed no one — "

An explosion drowned her crying. They clung to each other now, no longer playing their tragic roles . . . now they were just two frightened children. He squeezed his eyes tight shut, trying to wish everything into a bad dream. And then he felt gentle, old hands

separating them. He opened his eyes. A shimmercloak
rustled, blushed pink against deep blue. . . .

The Inquestor smiled. His sister's hand felt cold and
dry, like smooth stone. He released it.

The Inquestor said — his voice was so quiet, so
authoritative, "The Princeling's children. Why was I
not told?"

An underling's voice: "Lord Inquestor, we did not
know — "

"No matter. I am glad we have found them, and
they are alive. It would not have been compassionate,
to have abandoned them here . . . ."

"Let me die!" the girl cried.

The Inquestor only smiled. At last he said, "I cannot
do that. I cannot kill you without reason . . . no. I will
take you with me, assign you suitable clans, let you go
forth into the universe from which your world has
secluded itself for so many centuries." The boy could
hardly hear above the crackleroar of the burning city.
"Oh, do not be afraid, Kerin and Elloran, daughter and
son of Prince Taanyel. Don't try to follow your father
into a foolish death. . . . The Inquest is compassionate,
and will provide."

"It isn't fear that makes me cry," Kerin said. "It's
anger." The Inquestor had already turned his back on
them, expecting them to follow. "Loreh, Loreh," she
whispered, calling her brother by his child-name,
"don't ever forget what they did to us! Don't ever forget
who you are! They can't make us forget! Promise me,
even if we're separated by a thousand parsecs — "

Through his tears, the boy nodded. The smoke hid
her from sight. Death had spurned him, and now he
was all alone.

***

The Shendering system was unremarkable . . . there were hundreds of such backworlds in the Dispersal of Man. There was the little moon, now a sliver, but sometimes a pale peardrop, gleaming in the glitter-dark of the planet's night. The planet itself, cloud-shrouded, water-blue, its landmasses a startling green threaded with silver rivers and peppered with the fragments of the great vermilion road. The big moon, far off, pockish and jagged, where rockworms slithered, covering a millimeter a day and living off the cold light from the small yellow sun ... it was not a world to interest the great and powerful. "But a fine world," Tash Tievar said as the learning craft of the House of Tash made another pass over Shemberas, the Singing Mountains.

Some of the younger children gasped; Tievar could not suppress his smile. Once he too had seen his homeworld from space for the first time, when he had first been named to the Clan of Tash, the Rememberers . . . but that was eighty years ago. I remember too much, he thought, and turned to the business at hand. . . .

"Watch the world," he said. 'The children were silent, clustered in a semicircle on the mirror metal of the ship's floor; all the force- shields had been deopaqued, and it seemed that they floated on a mirror-disk in the midst of empty space. "Now, all together, eyes closed. . . ."

Eyes closed. Wringing remembrances from the inner darkness. The daily training of the clan of Tosh . . . "Good," said Tievar. "Now tell me what you saw."

Kerin, a highborn girl, displaced from her native world by an Inquestral war, for whom the Inquest had

found a home in the Clan of Tash out of their infinite
compassion, said, "Father Tievar, I remember the world
hanging between the two moons, three shells on a
peasant's necklace."

"Nice image. Your future master will like that."

"I don't want a master!" the girl cried out. Such an
outburst was not suitable, for all that Kerin might have
been a Princeling's daughter.

"Be careful," Tievar said as gently as he could. He
avoided her eyes, not wishing to single her out. The girl
had only been on Shendering for a few months, and
already she was his favorite. He turned to watch the
half-world wisped with hover-haze and wreathed with
a million stars, matching it in his mind with
remembrances of other worlds, other times ... "I know
you have endured much pain. The Inquestor who gave
you the name of Tash knew you would have
Remembering in you; because your father's suicide, the
destruction of your country, your world, would be
branded indelibly in your mind as a Rememberer's
Remembrance is branded . . . but there are also things
that a child of Tash must forget if she is to do what is
ordained . . . come, I don't wish to scold you. You are
doing well here." He watched the girl as she stood for a
better view; she wore the plain white tunic of the clan
of Tash well, as though it were a costly robe. If only she
knew how much I understand her pain, he thought. He
wished he could tell her about his love for her, how he
felt for her what a father feels . . . but it would not have
been right. The memory of another father still burned
inside her, and he knew better than to touch such a
remembrance.

Now all the children were doing their remembering
exercises, and the small craft sped swiftly from the
world, aimed at the greater of the two moons. They

resent this training, Tievar thought, because they believe they will never have to use it. But I have been Rememberer for an Inquestor once already. Only his death released me. And in all that time he called for me perhaps a dozen times. Powers of powers, what use are we really?

"Be ready," he called out. "We'll hit a displacement field in a few

minutes." Suddenly they were through; the perspective had changed in an instant. Now it was Shendering that was distant, a fierce crescent of blue fire behind the craggy rim of Dhaendek, the dead moon. A collective catch of children's breath . . . "The exercises. Don't forget why we're here."

"It must be so cold there," said Kerin. He thought he felt a twinge of longing in her voice. But she was too young, surely, to long for coldness. . . .

. . . and then the last moon, Kilimindi, hardly more than a rock, but within it, hollowed out of the dead basalt, the palace of the absentee Inquestor who governed the system. The little moon's surface was made smooth by the Inquestral architects, checkered with square fields of ice to look like a shtezhnat board warped into a sphere. Tash Tievar compared the images with his remembrances and found them true.

But now the children were clamoring for stories; and he wanted to remind them of the high seriousness of their purpose, so he went on with the lesson in earnest.

"Your services may never be required," he said, "but if they are ... if a time should come when, through a game of makrúgh, this planet must be destroyed . . . they will summon us. 'The Inquestors do not like to destroy planets, children. Their purpose is ... we cannot really understand it. To preserve the balance of the Dispersal of Man, to protect us from stagnation . . . but there is a House of Tash on every planet. We are all like aliens here, shunned because of what we represent. When war comes we will know first. The people of Shendering — as many as can be saved — will be packed into people bins and towed by convoys of delphinoid shipminds through the not-space between spaces, the overcosm, waiting, for centuries perhaps, for a new world to become available. But a few of us will be chosen, we who Remember. For every Inquestor who has taken part in the game of makrúgh must acquire one of us, to remind him — in perpetuity — of the planet that he has caused to die. . . . The Inquestors value compassion above all things. That is why we exist, so that they will never forget that they must have compassion." He stopped suddenly. He had seen something that did not accord with his remembrance —

Kerin was saying, "They don't seem to have learnt very much about compassion. I saw rivers of white fire gush through the city streets — "

But Tievar was not listening. He had seen something . . . something he hoped he would never see again in his life. A serpent-string of silver cylinders. Slowly they were circling the moon, flashing briefly in reflected light before the darkness swallowed them . . . and streaks of delphinoid ships, darting among them like corkscrew comets. No! Tievar thought. It can't be —

A chill shook him, a dread he had only felt once before in his life.

"I think," he said, "that the lesson is over. I think we should return to the world now, to the House, get a little refreshment . . ." his voice wavered. "We will be having visitors soon — "

A babble from the children. "Visitors, Father Tievar? Who?" Tievar closed his eyes, subvocalizing instructions to the craft's little thinkhive. The craft shuddered, shifted, did a momentary stomach-wrenching gravity change. The moon was behind them now. Tievar did not want to look back, but something impelled him —

"The visitors. Father! Who are they?" It was the girl Kerin.

"Inquestors." Even without looking he felt the girl freeze. She was Remembering her past. A world in ruins. Well, she would have to forget it now. They would all have to forget a great deal before year's end. . . .

"It's time, then! And I've only just come from one war-wrecked planet, to find that I must — "

"Do not weep, Kerin. You will not have time for weeping now. We'll all have to intensify the work, have longer Remembering sessions, more field work . . . there won't be much time."

"I am not weeping!" Kerin said defiantly, and Tievar decided not to look too closely.

Instead he watched the people bins. From this distance they seemed like little silver pellets, beads perhaps, a bracelet around the moon. . . . The starships stormed like phosphorflies. It was hard to believe that each people bin could hold millions of people, stasis-frozen and stacked in racks. . . .

What did they want with this poor, insignificant planet? What crisis in the Inquestral game of makrúgh had forced the war to move to this sparsely peopled quadrant of the Dispersal? Tievar watched the children. Many were silent, wondering about the future. Some were chattering with excitement. Perhaps they would be chosen! Perhaps they would live in an Inquestor's court!

"Father Tievar . . ." It was the voice of the girl Kerin.

"Yes?" She had drawn him away from the crowd of children.

"If you are chosen by the Inquest, will you go. Father Tievar?"

"I'm too old."

"So if they choose me. I'll never see you again?"

"Never. Because I will not go out again. I have been a Rememberer too long. The memories confuse me now, and I long for . . ." he did not want to say death, not aloud; it would frighten the child.

"I know what you mean, Father. I too have wanted to die. To crawl away to a place as cold and dead as the emptiness I've carried inside since Father's death. . . ." The girl frightened him sometimes. She was so intense, her past still burned inside her. She had not yet learnt that there are things a Rememberer must forget. And then the girl said, "I will never leave you."

He was moved, that she had touched him with her love. But he had nothing to say, no comfort, no platitudes of wisdom. So he turned to watch the people bins and said nothing.

***

With a flick of his mind. Ton Elloran n'Taanyel Tath dissolved his tachyon bubble and stepped out onto the surface of the doomed world. With him came Sajit, his musician, and a music of tinkle-topped sighs from strings of song-jewels that hung about their necks; for Elloran could go nowhere without music; he found the silence too painful. There were too many memories to be found in silence. Utopias destroyed.

Planets in ruins. And . . . when he thought too deeply ...
a memory of a small boy, waiting to die, in a dark huge
dreadful silence.

It was a forest clearing. In the grass, a few meters of
vermilion road, garish against the grass-green; a
displacement plate. For the only city on Shendering
was Jen, the Scrambled City, a city shredded into
minuscule jigsaw fragments and scattered all over the
landmasses, linked by a single scarlet road and by a
million displacement plates, the buildings artfully
concealed underground, under quilts of jungle
overhang, under umbrella-cliffs and ocean-floors . . .
whoever designed the city had not wanted to inflict
man's presence upon the planet's wildernesses. In Jen,
you dared not leave the road unguided for an instant,
or you would never find it again.

Now it was deepest night, and the only light was
the soft blushing of Elloran's shimmercloak, a pale pink
shifting across the deep blue shimmerfur. Another step
and it was a brilliant, flower-fragrant night with two
moons shining, a pocked moon and a haloed one. A
step later, bright daylight, mist-blue hills; another step,
twilight and a brook bridging the red road, winding
around boulder croppings . . . and always the landscape
peppered with white rosellas, the most prosaic of all
flowers. For a moment Elloran felt a sea- breeze,
breathed a sharp tangy smell, and then —

The road forked. Flicking an image of the city's
layout into his mind, Elloran saw where to turn and
what instructions to subvocalize into the next
displacement plate. Cliffs loomed, blurred into
meadows, meadows shimmerfaded into orchards
doused in the bitter fragrance of ripe krangfruit.

"Are we there yet?" Shen Sajit, the musician, said. "I mean the House of Tash. Although why you choose to come here yourself — "

In the pause, a rush of shimmerviol music. "I had to. Sajit, I had a reason to lose this game of makrúgh. This planet has something I've been looking for, for fifty years. . . ."

"For this you're letting it get destroyed?"

Elloran didn't answer. He was thinking of Kerin. How old would she be now? He tried to calculate what effect time dilation would have had on her. Inquestors lived long lives, travelled mostly by instantaneous tachyon bubble, while the common people could only achieve the effect of longevity through the accidents of relativity. . . . She must seem younger, he decided. An image of the burning homeworld came into his mind for a moment, but he cast it away. It was so long ago, and he had lived through so much. . . .

I am an Inquestor now, he told himself sternly. My compassion extends equally to all men. It was different for other humans, even ones, like Sajit, who might have been friends if Elloran had not been an Inquestor. For a few seconds Elloran debated whether or not he should tell his musician of the real purpose of their journey to Shendering. How he had searched the colossal mind of the thinkhive on Uran s'Varek until he had found his sister at last. They walked faster; a river flicked into view, a veldt speckled with rosellas, a half-house growing from a sheared-off rockface. Kerin . . .

The road branched; displacement plates glinted in the thick grass. Elloran selected a turn. Abruptly they were in the House of Tash. A central atrium with a kaleidotinted roofshield, the light-colors dartshifting through whispertrickling fountains, sending pastel ripples across monochrome holosculptures of ancient heroes ... a cool place, subtle and restrained. He could hardly hear the songjewels' music above the burbling water.

An old man in the white tunic of the Rememberers came to greet them. "Ton Elloran," he said gravely, "I am Tash Tievar, senior instructor here. You will give audience in this atrium?"

Elloran nodded. A hoverthrone of faded wicker materialized on the displacement plate at his feet. He ascended. "I suppose you know why we are here. The representatives of the Inquest, I mean."

"Who could fail to do so, my Lord?" Was there bitterness in the old man's voice? Powers of powers, I'm not responsible for the way our universe is!, he wanted to say. I didn't choose to be where I am now. . . .

"Know then," he said formally, "that war has come to this sector of the Dispersal of Man, and that in all probability the Shendering system will fall beyond . . . that in its compassion the Inquest has prepared people bins to receive such of this world's inhabitants who wish to avoid the possible annihilation of the world . . . and that I as spokesman of the High Inquest do solemnly invoke the charter of the Clan of Tash, to choose a rememberer for myself." This last he spoke in the high speech, according to formula.

"What selection process shall you require for the people bins?"

"Whatever selection plan was chosen when the world was first chartered."

"By choice, then, with those possessing clan-names having the right of first choice."

"Very well." What a tired, pointless ritual it seems! Too many times Elloran had spoken these words and consigned faceless millions to their deaths. But it is necessary! Man was a fallen being. To be static was to court a thousand heresies, worst of all the heresy of utopianism. War was necessary! It was the deepest of human instincts! At least, now, war was controlled by the Inquest; war was compassionate, striking only when it must. But to be an Inquestor was to court the most terrible of all lonelinesses. Elloran wondered if this old man understood the pain of it, the terrible war between guilt and compassion that every Inquestor strove to conceal deep inside himself.

    ***

Tash Tievar stood silent, waiting for another command. "The Rememberers. I must have Rememberers, Tievar. Twelve Inquestors took part in this game of makrúgh, and none must ever forget . . ." When was the last time he had summoned a Rememberer? A decade?

Next season, when I return to the palace . . .

"Pick whom you will. Lord Inquestor."

"Let lots be drawn, or use some other fair method. It doesn't matter to me. Except ..." he tried to keep his voice steady. "Except for myself. For myself I wish to requisition the girl named Tash Kerin."

Why had the old man turned so pale? "What's the matter?" Elloran said.

"My Lord — she is so new here, so untrained— I did not know that you Inquestors knew so much about us, knew our very names and the planets on which we were stationed — "

"Fetch her." There. It was done. The old man stepped onto a displacement plate and was gone into the next room. Perhaps the next room was on the other side of the planet; Elloran did not know how fine the scrambling of the city was.

He commanded Sajit to call forth an eerie music from the song-jewels, like the call of ancient cetaceans in the ocean of mythical Earth. It whined above the trickling of the iridescing waters. And suddenly she was there —

She didn't speak. She's so young —

"Kerin."

"Lord Inquestor?" Elloran saw a slip of a child, her blond hair cropped unbecomingly like a peasant's, her eyes wide, dark, fierce. She did not avoid his gaze the way commonfolk should. He was proud of her for this, for not forgetting who she had been.

"Kerin — you're so young, still — it must have been only yesterday for you, the childsoldiers ravaging the city, the burn-ing world, keeping death-watch over our father — "

And suddenly she knew. She shrank back from him. "You've become one of them! Loreh, you promised never to forget!"

"Kerin — " He reach-ed out, wanting to touch her, and it was as if she was in the past still, a ghost, taunting him, his fingers slipping through her . . . but it was only that she had darted behind one of the fountains. It gushed from the ceiling, defying gravity by means of a Shtoman varigrav device, cloaking her with spray-mist. "I know this is hard for you to accept, Kerin. I had no choice. They named me to the clan of Ton. They said that my past suffering would enable me to feel compassion. I had no choice!"

"You wanted to die! You grabbed the dagger from me, you were so eager!" Her voice was a shrill shriek, lost in the echoing rush of waters. She did not look at him now. She backed into the shadow of a huge holosculpt ta-bleau, her face criss-crossed by shadow-horns of a my-thical beast, her white tunic burning amber-mauve-em-erald in the light from the skyroof's kaleidolon.

"You don't know how I've looked for you."

"I don't care! You've killed our father all over again, you traitor — "

"I have a golden palace now. Its name is Varezhdur. The palace flies from star to star. I am a Kingling with a dozen worlds. I have worn the shimmercloak of the Inquest for fifty years, and all this time I have searched for you, and all this time your starship sailed the overcosm, with a half-century squashed by relativity into a single year ... I have told no one, not even Sajit whom I trust more than any man. . . . For you I played makrúgh, to get you back I picked this planet to die — "

"You don't look sixty years old."

"We never need to age. You can share this too, you can share all o fit—""You're an Inquestor. You can make me do any-thing. If you requisition my services as Rememberer I have no choice."

"I will not force you, Kerin." It had all been for nothing! Elloran clapped his hands for louder music, hoping to deaden his grief. Percussion thundered and thudded. "Isn't there any way we can start again?"

She came towards him then, disrupting the fountain and sending the spray flying. She was saying, "There is an old man here, a teacher, Tash Tievar ... he has been like a father to me. I have promised to stay with him always. To stay here, and perhaps be killed, if need be . . . I've been prepared to die ever since our world died at the hands of the Inquest. I will go wherever he goes."

"Then I will requisition him too. There's no problem there."

"You say you would not force one of us?" She laughed then, an angry, desperate laugh that he had never heard from her in all their childhood. She had changed so much. Again Elloran had the uncanny sensation that she was only an illusion, a shadow-revenant from the coffined past.

"No," he said, "I will not force one of you. Compassion is our way, not compulsion."

"Tash Tievar will not leave. Ton Elloran," said Kerin. "And so I will not leave; my honor binds me, and the Inquest, I know, understands honor well."

He stood speechless for a moment. In coming here, in revealing his emotions so nakedly, he had violated everything the Inquest had taught him. How could the Dispersal of Man be held together if even Inquestors ignored the trappings of degree, broke caste, pleaded with under-lings? He wanted to be a brother, not a Kingling dealing with a subject, but ... for him it had been fifty years. He had expected gratitude, not resistance. Not that Kerin would play makrúgh against him — and win! He had forgotten how alike they were.

"At least — at least — I'm your brother, Kerin — "

"I have no brother," Kerin said softly, bitterly. "My brother was killed by the Inquestors last year, the year they devastated my home world." And she walked back through the fountain, vanished from the displacement plate. From the song-jewels around his neck came a burst of mar-tial music, inanely cheerful.

There was still time, some days at least, before the war would come to Shendering. Tievar thought it was best to continue as he had always done. Today he led the children away from the road a little. They stood in an open field flecked with wild rosellas. The children clustered around him, wildflowers themselves, he was thinking. "Close your eyes now. Perceive the fragrances. Separate all the scents until you can enumerate them all, every blade of grass, every flower. . . ."

He took Kerin aside then. "You did wrong, little daughter, to mock the Inquestor, to link your fate with mine."

"I can't help it. Father!" And then she told him everything that had passed between her and Elloran. "How can I go to him now, knowing that he's callously killed this world to get me back?"

Tievar touched the girl's cropped hair for a moment. He did not know what to think. He was disturbed, that an In-questor would move a world to fulfill his own emotional needs. Inquestors were supposed to be beyond such things. And she is so like him, he thought, in her own way, dragging me as a pawn into her conflict with him ... he left her abruptly, turning his mind to the Remembering exercises. He had the children singing monotonous, mind-stilling chants now, lulling all the senses except for the sense of smell and the touch of the breeze.

Then, without warn-ing, a different music came—

Harsh resonanceless highwoods shrieking through waves of shim-merviol and whisperlyre like exotic fish skip-skim-ming the waves. It was Ton Elloran and his friend, the silent musician.

"My Lord—"

"Go on, Tash Tievar. It is not our intention to interrupt your little lessons." Uneasily, Tash Tievar muttered a few more instructions.

The apprentices were too rigid, too wound up by the Inquestor's presence, to be able to concentrate on Remembering. Pointedly Kerin took up a position as far away from , the Inquestor as possible, squeezed her eyes tight shut, feeling nothing but the wind and the fragrance.

Elloran did not seem to notice Kerin. Of course, Tievar thought, he would not go so far as to show his emotions to us, the shortlived. Instead, the Inquestor chose to ask questions about the planet, and about Remembering.

"The city," said Tievar, "is practically a m3d;h to most of the world's in-habitants. Who would no-tice a patch of vermilion in the middle of a hundred or more square klomets of countryside? And the city is well scrambled ... at times the road even touches the surface of the moon Dha-ëndek, where miners try to trap the rockworms for their crystalline sto-mach linings . . ." Tievar saw that Kerin was listening to every word, despite seeming to concentrate on her exercises. He went on, "Remembering is hard for most people. There are so many things that men would rather forget. But Rememberers are like the rosella flowers, Inquestor, which are so hardy they can subsist ansTwhere." He stooped, plucked one; it was a tiny thing with a thousand prickly-stiff petaloids. He crushed it; it was pulverized into a mil-lion spores, and he blew them into the breeze. "Each one seems so fragile, doesn't it? Yet it's been said they would bloom even on Dhaendek, living off the sunlight and drawing sus-tenance from the rocks, toughening themselves a-gainst the almost zero cold. Memories will come, no matter how we fear them . . . like the spores of the rosella, clinging to your shimmercloaks, even to the hulls of delphinoids as they breach the overcosm, until they find new flelds to bloom in . . . and in a day they are dead. But did you not see, as you came along this branch of the road, which alternates winter and summer with every step,

that there wasn't a land-scape without a few of them?
Even the moun-tainpeaks glassed in with cold?"

"You are a born Re-memberer," Elloran said. "A true
artist. You make the humblest things sound
beautiful ... if only you would come with us."

"Inquestor . . . Your sister has told me everything."
He noticed Kerin pricking up her ears. But he had to
say this! "Perhaps you were not a good Inquestor — "

He saw Elloran stiffen. "Please." He tried to stay
unruffled, even though such forwardness might mean
instant death. "But I see now that you are hu-man,
underneath it all. Because of this, and be-cause of the
way Kerin has linked her fate with mine ... I have
decided not to stay on Shendering and die ... I love the
girl. Lord Inques-tor, and I won't see her throw herself
away in a needless gesture. I am old and my life would
have been useless but for this."

"Thank you," said the Inquestor. Not a word more;
it would have been unseemly for him to ex-press
fulsome gratitude, Tievar knew. They turned to find
Kerin —

"No!" she was scream-ing. "First my brother and
now my second father — you've both betrayed me! — I
don't want any part of this miserable universe of
yours!" The children's chanting wound down to a
pathetic murmur. Tievar saw Elloran's face, ashen,
appalled.

There was a second of stasis, and then —

Kerin was sprinting for the displacement plate,
trampling across the mea-dow towards the taller grass
that concealed the vermilion road, now her head was
bobbing up and down in the wavy green —

She was gone. A cry escaped Elloran's lips. / pity
him, Tievar thought, and the thought was strange . . .

how could you pity a man who had calmly arranged for the destruction of your whole world?

"Quick! We must follow her — if she leaves the crimson path, there's no way we'll find her again — " he said.

They ran for the plate. 'The Inquestor and the musician and the old man. The children following in a huddle.

Touching the path —

Nightfall. A branch in the road. The girl's shape, shadowslim, flitting to the left.

Snow. Rainbows bridg-ing the mountainpeaks.

Summer. Beach. Au-tumn. Dead leaves freckled with rosellas.

Darkness. Jungle. Twi-light. Taiga. And then —

"We've lost her." Sajit the musician was speaking. They had run perhaps only a hundred meters down the road.

"Powers of powers!" cried Elloran. "Fifty years I've searched for her . . ."

Tievar was breathing heavily. He was too old for this. Through his ex-haustion he heard them talking —

"Her gene-pattem. Must be in the planetary thinkhive. They'll monitor all over the planet, surely they'll trace her. . . ."

Elloran. "No, Sajit. This world has no such amenities."

"We could use troops. We have enough extra ships crammed with child-soldiers."

"The war is due soon. It's hopeless."

"Inquestor — " Tievar spoke up. The two turned on him, waiting. "I am a Rememberer. Perhaps I may speak more freely than most. I know this world well — it is my duty — and I have known the girl these past few months as well as though she were my own daughter. Perhaps I can trace her. Let me try to find her. Ton Elloran. Give me a few days, set a deadline before you rain the fire-death on this world."

"Yes. Yes."

"Three sleeps then," said Sajit, taking his mas-ter's arm. Elloran said nothing; but he nodded once.

And Tievar said, "But — and I say this as Rememberer — you must realize that though you are Inquestor you are only a man. Man is a fallen being, is he not? Perhaps you will learn from this, that you cannot always get want you want, even though you bum down the moons from the sky." Powers! I don't mean to mock him. . . .

"You ignorant idiot!" the musician cried in a sudden passion. "Do you think he doesn't know this already? Do you think he isn't burning from the pain inside himself, from which he can never escape? Do you think the clan of Ton is for sadists and mass-murderers?"

Elloran still said nothing, but waved him to be silent.

The Inquestor and his musician stepped towards the displacement plate. In a second, Tievar and the children were in silence, for the music of songjewels was gone. Tievar and his apprentices stepped in a different direction. A blizzard, bitter-cold, assailed them. "Re- member this cold!" he shouted over the howling wind. "Remember it all .your lives!" He closed his mind to the cold, trying to think of Kerin and where she was likely to have gone.
***

Thousands of parsecs away, a golden palace danced against the stars as it orbited a rich world. There were wings and corridors and arches and towers and klomet-long comet-tail-streamers of beaten gold. And in the palace's heart, a throne-room. And in the throne-room, swirling slowly in an artificial lightfield, a galaxy made of dust. A dust-sculpture. It was the most private of Ton Elloran's thronerooms.

The tachyon bubble materialized, dissolved. Elloran and Sajit were alone together in the vast hall.

"I've failed!" Elloran cried. "Sajit, more music — "

"Wait." Elloran allowed himself to be helped into his huge throne, with its firefur cushions stuffed with kyllap leaves, with its wide steps of sculpt-friezed gold. He stared at the dust nebula. Years ago both he and Sajit had loved a dust-sculptress, but she had rejected both of them, loving the dust more. This galaxy of dust was their only remembrance of her. This old love, and many shared experiences, had forged an uneasy bond between the musician and the Inquestor, although one could hardly speak of friendship between two men so unequal. . . . Elloran wished, sometimes, that they could have been close friends, that he could have told everything long ago.

But it was not in the nature of things.

Sajit said, "Why did you try to do it this way? Why the game of makrúgh? Couldn't you just have sent a tachyon bubble for her and be done with it?"

"I've forgotten so much," Elloran said. "What it is to be a normal human, in utter terror and awe of the Inquest . . . it's been so long! I played makrúgh because it is what I'm used to, because to be devious has become second nature to me ... I thought she'd be impressed! That I had done all this for her! And now I've killed her!"

"Perhaps not. In three sleeps — " But Elloran would not answer.

With a wave of his hand and perhaps a subvocalized command, Sajit summoned a soft music of shimmerviols, the sweet voices of neuter children weaving and twining long wordless melodies. "Drown me in it!" Elloran whispered.

Sajit had come up with him to the throne. Even with his friend so near, Elloran felt terribly alone. "You should have told me," Sajit said. Elloran looked at his face, more aged than his own that had been frozen in an ageless youth. Inquestors did not talk about their past, about the time before donning the shimmercloak. It was so deeply ingrained ... an Inquestor must seem to have sprung from nowhere, like a god . . . couldn't Sajit understand? He could not rush in and acknowledge the girl to be his sister before a whole planet.

Such knowledge of an Inquestor's humanity could hurt the Inquest —

"Sajit, the Rememberers. All of them. Now. Order them awakened. Here, at once."

"Elloran—"

"Obey, curse you!"

Presently they came. It had been night in the palace of Varezhdur — night and day fell at the Inquestor's whim — and they were half-asleep, dazed at being admitted into the Inquestor's secret place. There were a hundred of them or more: old men and women, children, people in their prime, all with their white tunics hastily pulled on and their hair dishevelled and their faces streaked with sleepiness.

"Remind me!" said Elloran.

They began. They talked of a triple world, of a gas giant glowering in the sky through the silhouettes of tower-tall trees. Of a hot world with cool bubble-houses shadowed by smouldering sulphur-clefts. Of

water worlds where the humans built dark slimy
houses in the bellies of sea-serpents. Of beautiful
worlds, shimmering blue-green or russet or amethyst
in the void. . . .

"Remind me! Remind me!" Elloran screamed.

... of old men playing shtezhnat by the sea. Of
children with forcenets in the mountains, straining to
catch the leaping flamefish from volcanic lakes. Of a
young thief slipping into the shadows, clutching the
cut-off credit-thumbs of a dead merchant. Of bands of
women hunting for snow-phoenixes among the
glaciers. . . .

And Sajit was whispering to him, "Why torture
yourself more? Make it stop," and Elloran could see the
pain in the musician's face, but he couldn't stop—

... of last days. Of crisp-burnt birds raining onto the
fields. Of fire flushing corpses from the catacombs. Of
childsoldiers whirling blazing death from their
hoverdisks —

"Stop!" Silence fell.

Elloran remembered at last, that memory he had
tried to forget for fifty years. He did not weep; he was
too drained. The people of the clan of Tash stood
uncertainly, waiting for a new command.

REMEMBRANCES 71

"How long have I been listening?" he asked Sajit
weakly.

"More than a sleep, Inquestor." Sajit was always
careful to speak formally when they were not alone,
and Elloran was grateful for that. "They must be tired.
Lord Inquestor."

"Yes. Dismiss them." It seemed that he only blinked once, and they were gone. Phantoms, he thought. The past returning to haunt us — by our own command ... it takes a certain masochism to be an Inquestor. . . .

"I'll rest now," he said when he was alone with Sajit. "Command a soothing music for me. And after, after ... we will return to Shendering to see the end."

"Do you have to tor-ment yourself so?"

"I have no choices. I have relinquished all my freedoms. I am an Inq-uestor."

At dawn Tash Tievar rose and followed the vermilion pathway out to the field where he had last spoken to Kerin. The wind was gusting sharp, making the grass dance, churning up the dead rosellas. Even as his mind raced, trying to think where Kerin might have gone, he was drinking in the wind and the whis-pering meadow, fashioning a future Remembrance. . . .

He squatted on the grass, alone. At the House of Tash, the chosen ones were being readied; the rejected ones were already leaving en masse for the packaging houses to be prepared for the long joumey in people bins. He closed his eyes, making his mind blank, an empty message disk, as a Re-memberer must when he is preparing to summon up a vivid Remembrance. . . .

Kerin —

She had come to the House of Tash a girl on fire, yet speaking always of the bleak and cold. A memory surfaced like a sea-mammal hungry for air —

I too have wanted to die. To crawl away to a place as cold and dead as the emptiness I've carried inside since Father's death. . . .

He saw her as she said those words. In the learning craft, looking out into space. And then he saw —

Dhaendek, a dead rock whose shadow fell over Shendering, dead craters made glitter-faceted by borrowed light. It must be very cold there. The twinge of longing in the voice.

Tievar opened his eyes. At the zenith Dhaendek shone still, a moon-ghost softened by sunlight, half-hidden in amber dawnlight. The wind made a miniature hurricane of husked rosellas, freckling his hair and shoulders.

It has been said that they would bloom even on Dhaendek —

He roused himself. There were places when the crimson road went through caverns or underground chambers. There were places when you suddenly felt a stomach-twisting lightness for a moment, almost as though . . . they said that the pathway touched the moon, but only Rememberers, well-trained and cautious ones at that, would leave the pathway for the treacherous places beyond . . . Kerin was a good Rememberer. He had trained her well. She would have noticed.

Quickly his mind traced over the thousand branches of the road. The city's maps showed only what the city would look like if it were not scrambled; so long as you stuck to the road, you would not need to know the road's locations in true space. He would have to go by memory, by following the twists and turns in his mind until he recalled the queasy-making stretches of the road. . . .

Resolutely he turned now, stepping onto the displacement plate, subvocalizing instructions to its mechanism.

The light gravity hit him at once, and the chemical-rich odor of the air. The road — only three or four meters of it — was in total darkness; only the displacement plates at either end glinted. No walker along the road would have bothered to notice such an anomaly; it would have been dark, one would have pressed onward to one's destination. After a few minutes, when his sto-mach had stopped groan-ing, he left the road, bump-ed into a wall, groped his way along it for a while, found a door that ac-cordioned open when he touched the stud. . . .

A village square. Over-head, a roof of rock. Houses hewn from the living stone of Dhaëndek. A few people, dressed in rags, wandering about.

"Please could you tell me — " A woman saw him. She pointed. Screamed. Made some gesture to ward off evil. 'The square emptied abruptly. Tievar walked on. It must be a village of those who hunted the rockworms on the surface. 'The hostility he understood. The clan of Tash was evil-omened. No one wanted to see one now, when news of the world's end must surely have reached even Dhaëndek.

Mocking laughter. Tie-var whirled round —

A woman was watching him. She was middle-aged, swathed in a shapeless smock, grinning. "Cowards, the lot of them," the woman said. Her voice was raucous, grating on the nerves. "I know you're looking for the girl."

He started. "You've seen her?"

"Perhaps. A miner sees a lot, they say. You have to, to catch the worms before they notice you and lash you to smithereens."

"Where is she?"

"What's a cityman like you coming asking questions of us countryfolk that don't even know how to get to the city? I tell you. I'm not superstitious. I don't believe you whitecoats herald the end of the world. What would anyone want with Shendering, for powers' sake? Take the girl — "

"The girl! Quick! You'll be well paid."

"Keep your credit. I suppose you'll tell me to sign up for a people bin next. It's all a ruse, I say, to oppress us simple people. The girl . . . she stood here for a sleep, two sleeps, and everyone shunned her. Except me. Don't believe those stupid stories, I tell you. The chatter of hermaphrodites. I'm a miner with a clan name and I didn't earn it listening to nonsense."

"The girl!" Tievar said desperately.

"I took her where she wanted to go. Out in the middle of nowhere, past the last of the wormhordes. She was crazy, said it was time for her to die. Well, that's her business, and I only did her a favor."

"Take me there!"

"If the worms don't get us first." She laughed uproariously, thinking the prospect very funny.

The woman's name was Beren of the clan of Var. She led him down empty streets — Tievar got the feeling that they had only just become empty at his approach — and to a little rock-hollowed house where she threw him a pressure-skin and slipped herself into one herself. It was an organic, semi-sentient device that hugged his body, constricting but invisible save for the air-supply in its belt. A hoverplatform outfitted with strange gear waited on a displacement plate. Beren sprang up, beckoned him to follow, without waiting subvoked the command and they were on the surface —

Barren. Bleak. Craters within craters. Jagged mountains, a menacingly near horizon, and half-Shendering and distant Kilimindi shining dimly, casting soft twin-peaked shadows. And the silence. Tievar had never known such silence, even at the most profound levels of Remembrance-concentration.

They sped over the pocked, gravelly terrain. Now and then the floater mechanism kicked up a dust-flurry and the dust-motes took a long time falling. "Are there many rockworms here?" he sub-vocalized, hoping the skin had a conversing device.

"Ha!" a thin whisper in his ear. "We mine them . . . mostly they just sit and photosynthesize, hut if they sense danger they'll lash out once with their tails and . . ." Another laugh, converted by subvoking into a strange cough-grating sound. "If we get them right we spray them with liquid water," she tapped some of the strange apparatus on the floater, "and this freezes instantly and keeps them still long enough for us to slit their stomachs and gather the carbon crystals, huge ones the size of a baby's head — "

"Carbon crystals?"

"Diamonds. They come somewhere in the middle of their digestive chain — "

Tievar let the woman chatter on. Her mouth never moved, as his did by accident whenever he talked; he was not used to subvocalizing whole conversations. The tinny buzz of her speech continued; and he listened, because if he did not he would think of finding Kerin's corpse, lying frozen in a crater. He was terrified to think of it. And then —

A sliver of white, running out of a crater-wall's shadow —

"Kerin!" he cried out, forgetting the airlessness. There was no sound. But she must have picked up the subvocalization on her pressure-skin. She twisted around, saw the floater, ran —

The floater skidded over a stray rock, righted itself, Tievar propped himself against a railing, they raced towards her, he subvoked her name over and over, and then —

"Where is she?"

"In a shadow somewhere," the woman said. "Shall we go back? Her air supply will run out soon anyway."

"Kerin!"

And then, in his ear, a quiet voice. "It's no use. Father Tievar. I made a pact with my brother, and I'm going to fulfill it even if he never does, even though he has gone over to the other side. It's no use, no use . . ." He thought she was sobbing. "I'm going to do something beautiful first, though. In a few seconds I'm going to dissolve my pressure-skin. Didn't you once say that the rosella might bloom even here, in the coldest land? Yet the people who live here wouldn't think of testing out such a theory. But a million spores are clinging to my body, to my clothes. I give them to this dead world, a gift from my dead heart."

He saw her darting out of the shadow —

"No!" he screamed, his voice helpless in the big silence. "She's going towards that glacier," he subvoked to Beren.

"That's no glacier! There's no glaciers on the surface, you ignorant cityman — that's a — "

A rockworm was slithering down a craterwall. It was like a crystal tunnel with a thousand icy segments. It was a hundred meters long or more. And Kerin was running straight towards it.

And the floater was off! Rising with a suddenness that toppled Tievar onto the platform, racing towards the rockworm. And then Tievar saw the creature's innards through its transparent exterior, quivering, shivering constructs of tubes and globules like an ancient chemist's laboratory, and the octahedral diamonds, fist-huge, rolling slowly around . . . "Kerin!" he tried to shout. How could she not notice —

A scream, transmuted by the skin's device into a strangled whistle —

The tail, coiled on the other side of the crater wall, whipped out. Kerin sailed upwards —

"Quick! Do something!" But Beren had already commanded the floater. It sprang up, swerved to avoid the backlash; Tievar saw Kerin falling, slowly, slowly in the moon's low gravity, and then —

The monster reared up, glittering, he saw crystal plates rippling slowly, the inner organs pulsating crazily —

"If she's already opened her pressure skin," Beren said quickly, "open yours. Seize her, tight, hold her to your opening. The skin may adjust to hold you both —
"

'They soared! Tievar felt a stab of terror as they crashed the creature, pry-ing loose a shower of cry- stalrock, and then swung away to avoid —

Curve of the crystal tail, then —

A hundred nozzles, spraying mist over the creature! Making it shudder to a standstill, crusting the crystal surface with fine ice —

Kerin, crashing onto the speeding floater. "All in a day's work," said the miner. But Kerin —

"Something's wrong with her!" Tievar clasped her to himself. 'The skin was undone. At once he dissolved the skin that was hugging his chest, clutch-ing the girl to him. Her eyes were stiff and open as if in death. The cold of vacuum seared him for a moment, and then the skin grew taut around them both. He felt cool blood wetting his chest. She had only been exposed to the vacuum for a few seconds, but a little while longer and . . . "Kerin . . ."

She did not speak. The floater came to rest a few centimeters above ground, and Var Beren was already seizing the opportunity to slice open the immobilized rockworm. The vibrosaw was efficient, spewing crystal guts and diamonds all over the stony ground. And Kerin was stirring. . . .

"Why are you punishing me?" clasped together in the same pres- sure skin, they could speak to each other now.

"You were punishing yourself, Kerin. Sometimes we see people only as what they represent. Your bro-ther was a symbol of those who had dispossessed you, who had driven your father to suicide. But he did not do those things, Kerin. It is Dispersal of Man itself, the order of things, that causes such things to happen. . . ."

"I don't believe it," Kerin whispered. "I can't accept that things must be as they are. I want to fight them, I want to destroy them — "

"Understand yourself," said Tievar. "You think you ran away because you were angry — at me, at Elloran. But you can't punish the universe by killing yourself. That's a child's way. And you are fast becoming a woman, Kerin. This is the only universe we will ever have. You have made a beautiful gesture worthy of a Rememberer, but now you must understand why you tried to destroy your-self. . . . It's because you were angry at you, not us. Because, with all your hat-red of the Inquest, you could not bum away your love for your brother." She did not answer him, but he knew that it was true. He held the girl tightly, shielding her. And then she pointed towards the dead rockworm, to where Beren was approaching with a forcenet stuffed with dia-monds that she would never be able to sell now, she pointed feverishly until he saw what she wanted him to see —

In a cleft between two rocks, some meters away, a rosella was budding. They wasted no time, those hardy little blooms, adap-ting to anything. Tievar smiled sadly, storing the Remembrance; but Kerin's face held no expression at all.

Kilimindi. The strong-hold of Ton Karakael, ab-sentee Kingling of Shen-dering and a score of other systems.

A huge arena-hall, a disk englobed by force-shields that let in the starlight. Its floor appeared to be dark blue grass; in fact it was carpeted with the living fur of shim-mercloaks, and now and then it would blush pale pink against the ultra-marine. A dozen Inquestors and their guests had ga-thered here. There were fluttering shimmercloaks, there were three-tiered headdresses topped with still-living featherskins cloned from peacocks and calliopteryxes, nude her-maphrodites with kohl-blackened eyes and nipples rouged with paste of pow-dered rubies.

Elloran had not wanted to come to this grand display; but his absence would have been unseemly. And the music of Sajit had been demanded; he could not, in all propriety, have failed to oblige, since it would have been com-mented on if he had shown rancor at losing a game of makrúgh.

It seemed a very artistic notion — to organize the disposal of the people bins into a grand fireworks with music. After all, once the planet's millions were in their temporal stasis, nothing could affect them at all — why not use them to make pretty effects? They would never know of the indignity they had suffered, when they awakened a century or two from then, on a new and perhaps hostile world.

Elloran looked over the familiar scene. He didn't want to play this game any more.

A thought touched him. One day the Inquest will fall ... he flicked it aside. He dived into the throng, mak-ing trivial conversations, feeling the awful aloneness that all Inquestors feel.

Sajit's music began: a sennet of a thousand brass-es, relayed from an audi-torium in the palace of Kilimindi. The room they were in began to move away from the moon; the conversation was stilled for a split second, and then continued as though nothing had happened.

And then Elloran saw the people bins. Their tops funnelled in readiness.

"Number one," the announcer said. "Exploding flowers." A swath of light played over the blackness. And suddenly it was full of people! Time-frozen in foetal position, scattering like dustmotes in a wind . . . the people bins swooped now, scooping them up like chaff, meiking swift swerving passes by the arena so the Inquestors could have a better view —

"It's beautiful, so beautiful, is it not?" said a young woman in a shimmercloak. He knew her to be Ton Zherinda, newly elevated to the Inquest. He nodded abstractedly. It was beautiful — and he needed beautiful things around him now, so that he might forget that he had murdered his sister, his birth-matched bride —

"Number two: phosphorflies over the mountains of Jerrelahf. . . ."

The light-swath darkened now. A new explosion of frozen people, this time each one coated with glowstuff, so they were like human meteors pelting the darkness, and now the people bins extended klomet-wide nets and swooped down to catch them as they flitted by. Thunderous applause now; everyone chattering wildly, wanting to know the name of the artist so that he could be engaged for the next game of makrúgh.

The Inquestrix, hardly a woman yet, still stood by him. Perhaps she was not yet at her ease among these jaded people.

"Vultures," he said. "Vultures!"

"What do you mean. Lord Elloran? Are you insulting these people as a means to begin a new round of makrúgh?"

"'No! I—"

And they were clus-tering around him now. "No!" he said. "I don't want to play now — "

"Brilliant!" an old man was saying. The Inquestors circled round, ignoring the fireworks now, while the rest still watched them in awe. "To begin a game by protesting a lack of desire to play — "

He was trapped. He looked for a way to escape. There must be a way to break the circle —

And then the announcer said, "A craft is ap-proaching. The display will begin again shortly. A craft of the House of Tash is approaching.

Inquestors muttered among themselves; the guests grumbled, com-plaining about the inter-ruption. In a few moments they were materializing on the displacement plates. Each one was in a fresh white tunic. Each one found the Inquestor to whom he had been as-signed and went directly to him. Suddenly there was silence. And, in whispers that were meant to be heard only by their masters, each Rememberer began to tell the story of Shendering. Outside, little towcraft whisked by, gathering the stray frozen people that the big bins had missed: for the fireworks were an aesthetic event, not a murdering one.

Elloran waited. Already the mood of jaded ex-hilaration was gone. Some of the Inquestors had gone off to far parts of the room with their Rememberers, brooding, moved. It was in these ways that the Inquest tried to discourage the pride that came with awesome power, the hubris of almost-godhood.

***

And then there was Tash Tievar. . . .

Elloran ran to the dis-placement plate, ignoring all seemliness. When Tievar stepped off the plate, she was there.

She came to him. She began to whisper in his ear as the others were doing, but he waved her silent.

They turned to watch as the people bins drifted away. Behind them was half-Shendering, heart-breakingly lovely, doomed.

"Don't say anything, sister," said Elloran softly. "'The Dispersal of Man is a brutal universe, and if we believe in it completely we will be crushed, like insects, like rats, like star sys-tems . . . but we are humans, and they cannot crush us completely, they cannot crush love. . . ." He did not dare touch her.

She was the ghost that had haunted him these fifty years. Now the two sides of his life were one, master and victim, and he could no longer tell which was which.

At last he remembered the past without pain.

She did not smile. Instead she reached into her tunic and handed him something.

A rosella.

He stared at it for a long time. Then he cupped his hands and crushed it and blew the spores out into the chamber. He thought he saw her eyes laugh a little.

Then he said, "Full circle. Again we keep deathwatch together."

And he hugged her hard to him, bursting with bitterness and joy.

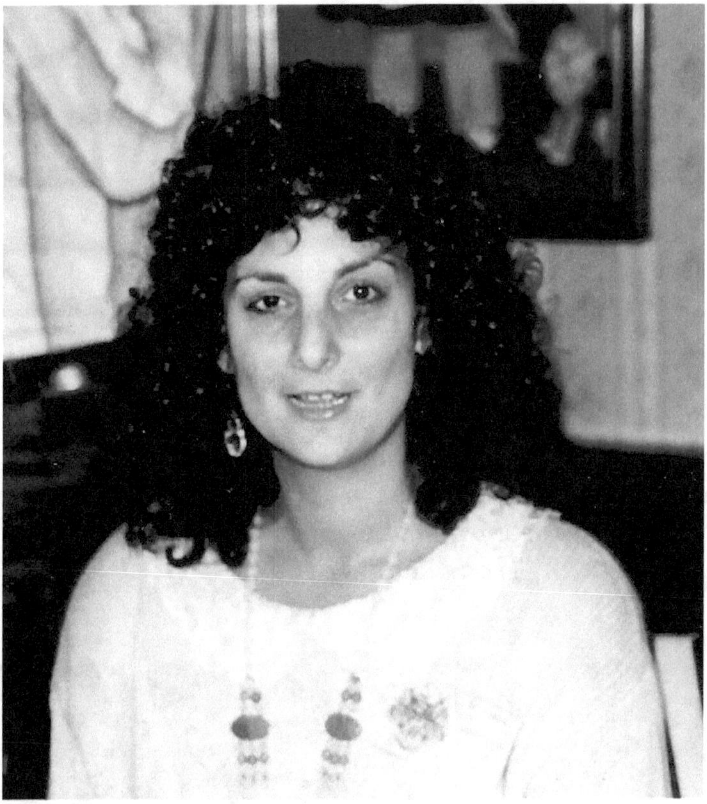

photo of the highly influential editor Ellen Datlow, *from the 1980s. Ellen edited Omni, the first "upmarket-looking" magazine devoted to science fiction.*

from Omnivisions

Twenty Years Ago ...

Edward Bryant and friends talk to Somtow on Ellen
Datlow's *Omnivisions*

Here is something really rare: the transcript of a chat
between the late Ed Byrant, Ellen Datlow and others
and me, from many many years ago. Here's a picture
of Ed Bryant from when he appeared in my classic of
risible horror, *The Laughing Dead.*

ED BRYANT

Good evening, everyone, and welcome to tonight's OmniVisions with our special guest, S.P. Somtow. I'll be having a bit of conversation with Somtow for the first hour; then producer Ellen will open up the chat to all who care to participate. So be preparing some stumper questions for tonight's extraordinary guest! S.P. Somtow's been publishing books in the sf and fantasy fields since the early '70s, starting with STARSHIP & HAIKU. As well as his novels, readers have taken note of his marvelous short stories, mostly recently collected in THE PAVILION OF FROZEN WOMEN. Some of his best-known works include the Timmy Valentine series, the latest volume of which is VANITAS, a continuation of his examination of vampirism.

SOMTOW

Well, the late 70s really ... my first pro pub was 79.

ED BRYANT

Also note the epic historical western lycanthropic novel, MOONDANCE. Somtow's a gifted composer who most recently premiered his royal-command ballet KALKI in Bangkok. He has directed two feature films, THE LAUGHING DEAD and ILL MET BY MOONLIGHT. His newest books are a young adult novel, THE VAMPIRE'S BEAUTIFUL DAUGHTER (Atheneum), and DARKER ANGELS (Gollancz and Tor). Welcome, Somtow!

SOMTOW

STARSHIP AND HAIKU was '81 ... I ain't that old to paraphrase chief Dan George, my hero. What a boffo intro, Ed, I am stumped! Ed is too modest to point out that he starred in both my films. The ballet is KAKI -- KALKI was by Gore Vidal, though oddly enough that book is

dedicated to Kukrit Pramoj, ex prime minister of Thailand and
plagiarizer of John Wyndham

ED BRYANT

Okay, okay, so I'm subject to typos. Let's start with DARKER
ANGELS. I just read British critic Simon Clark's review in SFX, in
which he said the novel is a "fascinating, awe-inspirting book, and
certainly the best I've read this year." That's heady stuff. I've read the
novel too and my opinions are pretty positive too, but let me ask you--
do you consider this a horror novel? Or a historical work? A dark
fantasy? A Civil War novel? E.L. Doctorow meets Stephen King? How
would you describe it?

SOMTOW

Well, Ed, if we must play the X meets Y game, I would say, OLDEST
LIVING CONFEDERATE WIDOW TELLS ALL meets NIGHT OF
THE LIVING DEAD. It has a similar structure to Alan Gurganus, with
the layered stories (his are consecutive, mine inside one another) ... the
actual analog is THE ARABIAN NIGHTS, though, as far as narrative
structure ... but no: NOT a horror novel really. I take that back. If you
take horror in a line from Henry JAmes and Hawthorne, then I'd say the
book could be considered horror, but it's not horror a la King, really ... it
doesn't have scared people running away from things. Simon Clark
really liked the book didn't he? "Best I've read all year" is the Holy
Grail in book reviews ... I've never received it before from anyone.
Remind me to pay him off!

ED BRYANT

Considering the setting, it'll be interesting to see if the book stays in
perpetual sale at gift shops at all the Civil War battlefields. The
beginning, in which the widowed Paula Grainger visits the body of the
recently murdered Lincoln lying in state, and then meets Walt Whitman,
is a stunner. I was intrigued by the structure you quickly establish, with
a succession of distinctive character voices telling the story. Did you
have to research this aspect, particularly the white Southerners and the
blackcharacters?

SOMTOW

I did study 19th century Black English as a foriegn language, and I also
taught myself Haitian creole which has a very similar except with
French vocab. Now Thailand is south of Mason-Dixon, but I dont
consider that a prequalification. However, I lived in Virginia for 7 years.
I am used to doing a lot of esearch on my historcial novels. In fact in
the excerpt thats on OMNI's page right now, you'll note certain recipes
that are from a wartime booklet circulated fior Southern housewives to
deal with ingredient shortages....

ED BRYANT

As a writer born and reared in Thailand, educated in Europe, and now
settled in southern California, you seem to be at ease in any number of
cultural environments. Do you have a particular interest in historical (or
contemporary, for that matter) Americana? I'm thinking not just of
DARKER ANGELS, but of other examples such as MOONDANCE.

SOMTOW

... but much of the research I did on MOON DANCE proved useful
here, since it is only 20 years earlier ... had to be VERY careful about
that though. Women's fashions were totally different in the 1860s from
the 1880s. Yes, Ed, I love 19th century America. It has a lot in common
with 20th.century Southeast Asia ... unbridled opportunity and
opportunism, sexual prudery comingled with incredible sexual
aberration ... In fact, I love many things about America than most
Americans might decry ... the tackiness ... the brashness ... as well as
the things Americans are proud of.

ED BRYANT

In this increasingly conservative U.S. cultural climate of the late '90s,
do you foresee getting any static for your temerity, for "cultural
appropriation"?

SOMTOW

Yes. Already got some heat for JASMINE NIGHTS. Why? Because it is a society of rich, privileged Asians, and the American characters are not great white father types but shown as comparatively underprivileged and declasse ... and how dare a little yellow boy have anything to say about American civil rights? But you know, I haven't REALLY had much heat from mainstream America for daring to write about middle class white people ... and I have had to study them just as much as I had to study the idiom and societal structures of native Americans or 19th century slave cultures.

ED BRYANT

How is your work received in Thailand?

SOMTOW

Interesting question, Ed. I'm a big celebrity there, do all the talk shows, am a notorious gadfly ... but not much of work has been read. All of it that's available was translated by my mother -- BRILLIANTLY "ported over" to an extremely alien linguistic matrix -- maybe 3 books, a dozen stories. I love being the sort of Howard Stern of Thailand, but ... it's hard to have a deep discussion of my work there without more of it being available

ED BRYANT

I'm curious about that very early work in Bangkok of yours that inspired Shirley MacLaine. Has that ever been reprinte din one of your own books?

SOMTOW

Aha! I was only 11 then so ... yes, I was forced to reprint it in FIRE FROM THE WINEDARK SEA, my RARE first collection. Do you know that Maclaines book has never gone out of print and that my poem has been seen by more people than have read all my other books put together?

ED BRYANT

True what I remember...that MacLaine thought your poem was the work
of some old and revered Thai classic author?

SOMTOW

"I am not a man" was a line from this poem. Natural thing for a kid to
say, but viewable, from a non gender specific ancient sage context, as a
highly feminist remark. The $500 I got in 1970 was the highest word
rate I ever received in my life....

ED BRYANT

Your other brand-new novel, THE VAMPIRE'S BEAUTIFUL
DAUGHTER... How would you describe it?

SOMTOW

... you want an X meets Y description? How about the dark side of
Buffy?

ED BRYANT

Nah--I'm not a producer you're pitching to. More of a reader-friendly
description... Tho the dark side of Buffy is something that will draw
ME to pick the story up!

SOMTOW

It's a kid's book ... just selected by the Junior Library Guild, so it is even
now corrupting the young of America. A half-Lakota, half-Jewish boy is
having an identity crisis, but meets a half-human, half-vampire girl at
Claudette Colbert High School in Encino (the setting for all my kids
books). They then have to learn the old WHO THEY ARE thing. It's
pretty touching I think. Oddly rnough, THE DARK SIDE OF BUFFY
is how director Mary Lambert describes "VAMPIRE JUNCTION," and
we're in the process of "taking meetings" even now on it ... its been on
and off for seven years, but THIS time I have high hopes.

ED BRYANT

This is not your first YA book--you've got a good track record. Any more on tap? Any any more adult historical off-trail novels planned?

SOMTOW

Thats about 20 Qs all at once really. Yes, I have an endless supply of YA novels up my sleeve ... if this one proves popular. (I've written 4; 3 have won some kind of award or received some honor). As for off beat historical novels ... boy, do I have one for you! I am doing a book called MOTHER OF GOD: THE MEMOIRS OF MIRIAM OF NAZARETH. In fact, if you want to throw this open to the floor, I believe that the Very Rev. Worley is itching to say something about this book .. as one of the few to have read the first 111 pages. But it is very subversive ... it explains the pagan roots of Christianity very explicitly.

ED BRYANT

Hmm. Is that going to raise as much...er...holy heck as I might guess it could?

PROFESSOR WORLEY

Hello, I'm Lloyd Worley, Prof. of English at Univ. of No. Co.The Mother Mary novel in progress is a stunner in many ways. There will be some Christians who will be shocked...yet, Somtow has brought a fine tune to his characters...who are both natural and INTERESTING! Both Mary and Paul are fascinating. I find that Somtow is one of the best...if not the best...stylist writing fantasy fiction today. What is a major influence on that style?

SOMTOW

Rev. Worley, my influences are very eclectic. But I would say that on the whole I've skipped the 19th century ... and seem to hark back directly to the 18th and earlier. As an English professor, do you see that? I'd say that my work is sort of influenced by Thomas Browne as disciplined by Jane Austen.

WORLEY

Yes, what I see is the 18th c. understanding of English as a kind of
symphony of sound. No short sentences, but no confusing sentences,
either. Lovecraft was successful at it, but he didn't have your ear.

ED BRYANT

Perhaps there's something to the observation that Somtow's music
informs his writing. And he IS an accomplished composer and
performer.

SOMTOW

I appreciate your comments about my ear; i HEAR everything I write ...
my first career was in music.

WORLEY

Yes, the "pagan roots" thing will terrify some people. Yet, even St.
Augustine recognized the value in pre-Christian ideas, ritual, and
practice. Thus, only the ignorant (as usual) will be angry and unhappy.

SOMTOW

Well said about the pagan roots. As always, those who haven't imbibed
at the Pierian Spring will be more furious than those who have (if you'll
excuse the Popish reference) I've been sneaking back into music ... in
fact, you should all run out and buy my CD KAKI from Tower Records

WORLEY

I think it's the music background that really informs Somtow's writing.
The KAKI CD makes for interesting background while reading
VANITAS...even though it's not written for it.

ED BRYANT

A good recent example would be the score for KAKI which is, I believe, available on CD. Where can people find it?

SOMTOW

Tower Records or: www.imaginaryrecords.com

ED BRYANT

Is there any of your other music available? Well, on the videos of your films, true?

SOMTOW

— and for a detailed exegesis of the MARY book, I invite the readers to check out this interview at the following website:

http://members.aol.com/tarotforum/feature.html.

Actually, how to get hold of almost everytihng I've done that is available is told in the MALLWORLD section of my web page: http://www.primenet.com/~somtow/somall.html

WORLEY

But for Somtow, it isn't only the music, it's his background in the humanities that also informs his writing. The Mary novel is interesting in that respect: first, it presents ancient Middle East people...who speak in modern English...yet this is not noticed by the reader. There's a feat! Not accidental, either, since Somtow is perfectly capable of controlling the speech of his characters.

ED BRYANT

Is the MARY book still in progress? And has the publishing world started to either express interest or recoil in shock?

SOMTOW

The Mary book has just been submitted to people. Got a great rejection
letter from Doubleday! Too controversial for them to publish! hohoho,
that letter is a framer. When the Rev Worley debates the Rev Falwell on
Larry King, the sparks shall fly!

WORLEY

Back to DARKER ANGELS. I first heard Somtow read the first chapter
to this book at a con in Ft. Collins, Colorado. The audience sat utterly
silent as he read...then insisted that he continue on to the second
chapter! Again, what the listeners were hearing was first-rate writing
and pure language control.

SOMTOW

Interestingly, the Pope is now considering deifying the Blessed Virgin.
In the year 2000 perhaps. This will change the very roots of
Christianity, the gulf between catholics and protestants will be
permanent, if it happens

WORLEY

The Virgin Mary has been considered an embodiment of the Holy
Ghost for quite a while, now, so a formal statement regarding this will
not be amiss, either among the Latin Catholics or the Eastern
Orthodox...who have a saying: "He who rejects the Mother will
eventually reject the Son."

TOWNSEND

Actually, the complete URL for Imaginary Records is
www.imaginaryrecords.com/~townsend. It's a lovely text-only
document; if a few folks order the "Kaki" CD (or Somtow's other
Imaginary release, "Hexaphony," I can buy a scanner and zip it up!
(Lloyd Townsend, Prop., Imaginary Records)

ED BRYANT

"Hexaphony"? Hadn't heard of that before. What is it?

SOMTOW

Thank you Lloyd. Whoops! Everyone on here is named Lloyd, right? Yes, please order the CD from the very courageous Lloyd Townsend ... he is a Card! HEXAPHONY was an improvisatory piece, sort of fusion meets post- serialism. 1977 vintage. It was world music before World Music ever existed as a category.

ED BRYANT

Somtow, recently a new edition of Ray Garton's LIVE GIRLS included a CD sound track composed specifically for the novel. Have you considered doing that sort of specific accompaniment for any of your books? Out in the mainstream, Judy Collins did it for her first novel. Maybe...maybe for MARY.

SOMTOW

What a splendid idea, Ed! I think I may do it! Please note that my music publisher is present here, so it is a good moment to plan new CDs!

ED BRYANT

You might say it'd be going for the full monty... Have you looked ahead of the MARY book? How many projects ahead do you plan and work? One at a time? More more of a carrousel of projects?

UNKNOWN GUEST

What an idea! Music to read the Valentine series by...this you must do! Ed's right on target.

SOMTOW

I am planning a third historical "horror" novel ... HANGMAN'S HOLLER. It isa novel in the CARNIVAL mode (like Blind Voices or Something Wicked or Lao). Set in 1899/1900 ... a millennial book ...

about TWO carnivals competing for the soul of a small Kentucky town ... with characters from the VJ series, Moon Dance, AND Darker Angeles in cameo. All dark fantasists thave a carnival book inside them! The dreaming jewels ... GOD what a brilliant book!

ED BRYANT

Yep. I'd certainly add William Lindsay Gresham's NIGHTMARE ALLEY to that list of cool dark carney books. How about film? Have you any plans fo returning to feature film or TV?

UNKNOWN GUEST

That's because carnivals aren't really fun...they're scary, creepy, and flavored with a touch of evil.

TYLER JOHNSON

What a great storyline! Any idea on a date of completion?

SOMTOW

Of 20th cent writers, STURGEON is my biggest influence. Not sure Tyler ... btw thanks for your email ... I love getting praise in my email box from peopple i don't know, makes it all worth while.... late 1998 probably. As for film ..well, I have been kinda burned lately, but the VAMPIRE JUNCTION project actually looks promising. As for my own films, gotta wait for more money. if I can repay the investors on ILL MET, I can make another film for sure.

ED BRYANT

Your literary influences are eclectic. How about musical? And filmic?

SOMTOW

You have found my secret, Ed. I am the ultimate magpie. The KAKI score: What if Prokofiev had spent a weekend on Bali? is how I saw it ... as for my films ... there's a kind of Italian sensibility to them maybe ... Fellini meets Tobe Hooper

TOWNSEND

Is "Mallworld" OP, or between printings? Do you plan to eventually revisit that universe, or produce any other "hard" SF?

Or another way of putting it--what have you listened to lately, or watched on screen, and genuinely enjoyed?

SOMTOW

MALLWORLD! Well, I wrote a new MALLWORLD story for THE ULTIMATE ALIEN .. as for SF, I have been feeling a little SF-ish lately, as far as doing short fiction in a near future ... I've done 2 stories like that in the last 3 weeks ... not sold them yet... Oh! I almost forgot! Stephe Pagel wants to do a "complete" Mallworld limited edition from his small press ... we have been talking about that.... if that comes through i will definitely do a few new MALLWORLD stories ... I have offered to do a novel-length sequel, but no one seems to want it ... yet.... Dead silence greets this revelation!

WORLEY

No silence from me...I eagerly await a complete edition of MALLWORLD stories...esp. from a small press. To clarify...the small press usually does a fine job of printing and binding....

SOMTOW

Yes Rev Worley, it would be a lovely book.

TOWNSEND

That was me asking about "Mallworld." When the complete edition comes out, tell Stephen I'll trade him a couple of Somtow CDs for a copy! Lloyd Townsend.

ED BRYANT

We've got another 10 minutes or so, so there's still plenty of time to proffer questions. Don't forget to sign them, please. Somtow, this is an incredibly standard question, perhaps, but not one I've ever heard you address. New and/or young aspiring writers tune in to OmniVisions. What advice would you pass along to these people?

SOMTOW

My advice to young writers is this: DO NOT BE AFRAID. That is what I have learned over the last 20 years. Say absolutely what you mean and really say it. No matter how much you want to skirt the issue. Being fearless is my secret ... such as it is ... I always go all the way....I never cheat my readers by teasing them and not delivering.

WORLEY

True...Somtow always follows through completely, as my students in Gothic Lit class discover when they read the Valentine series!

SOMTOW

Yes Lloyd, that's why some find it hard to stomach my books ... but they are honest.

ED BRYANT

So where would you like to see yourself in another 20 years or so?

SOMTOW

Yikes, Ed, I'll probably be dead in 20!

ED BRYANT

Nope, Somtow, you still have too many complacent readers and editors to stir up. You'll be around in 20.

WORLEY

Nonsense! Somtow has a long and productive life ahead of him! For those of us who love beautifully written dark fantasy, be grateful!

SOMTOW

...but I'll tell you what i'd like ... the Nobel Prize in literature. I mean, it is so damn political. At some stage, Thailand will have to have its turn, and then I'll be the only candidate. How's that for ambition?

JOHNSON

There is nothing more refreshing than an straight forward author who is not afraid to tell it like it is!

SOMTOW

Thanks a lot Tyler! .

ED BRYANT

It's a brash and--well, American sort of ambition. Just as you described much earlier... Somtow, thanks so very much for appearing on OmniVisions tonight. And to the rest of you, check out THE VAMPIRE'S BEAUTIFUL DAUGHTER from Atheneum, and DARKER ANGELS right now from Gollancz, and in Feb. from Tor. If you joined us late, scroll back to get web and e-mail locations to order Somtow's CDs, and to find his web site and fan club page. And thanks to producer Ellen, to questioners Tyler and the Lloyds, and to all the rest of you. Again, check in next week for Jim Freund's talk with Patrick O'Leary. Good night, and all of you have great holidays!

SOMTOW

Thanks to all, and good night! This has been a vigorous 2 hours!

DATLOW

Thanks Ed, Somtow, and everyone who came to watch and ask questions. I won't be in town to sys-op next week. Rob Killheffer will do so. I'm off to Spain.

SOMTOW

have a great time, Ellen!

Followup 20 years Later:

Ed asked where I would be in twenty years and I said dead. Alas, I've outlived Ed, one of the most brilliant, kind, and perspicacious people I've ever known.

All the web addresses listed in the interview are long defunct.

I still haven't won the Nobel Prize in literature, something predicted by Owen Lock in the late 1970s. His reasoning — well, I echoed it in the chat.

Some of the novels in progress never got written.

The Comet That Cried for Its Mother
by S.P. Somtow

Original Intro from AMAZING

This story is set in Sucharitkul's "Inquestor" universe, which has been the subject of numerous short stories and two novels so far, Light on the Sound *and* The Throne of Madness, *both available from Timescape.*

Millennia hence, the vast array of worlds known as the Dispersal of Man is overseen by the Inquest, a semi- religious elite motivated (supposedly) by compassion to prevent stagnation of the species by destroying "utopias" and forcibly reminding mankind of its fallen state. Whole planets are destroyed and populations displaced in the course of vast games of *makrugh* which no one, even the Inquestors, fully understands. Somtow has explained that the idea was to create a universe of extreme beauty and cruelty; and, while there are some similarities to Cordwainer Smith's universe of the Instrumentality, he points out that "his is more Oriental than mine." Perhaps an Inquestor can explain. We can't.

*****

. . . the child's eyes, amber-clear, deadly . . . "When I
die, hokh'Shen, *I want to be a comet."*
***

"A comet." Shen Sajit, wrapping his kaleidokilt around his waist and readying his array of musical instruments for the second half of the concert, watched the childsoldier they had assigned to guard him: lithe, slender, the black hair matching exactly the midnight of his tunic, the short cloak thrown sharply over his shoulder at just the regulation angle, the gravi-boots, iridium-laced, glistening. "Why a comet, boy?"

"Because they experience the tumblejoy. Master Musician, when they appear in a planet's sky as harbingers of the fire-death."

"You've lost me. Things have changed since I was a boy here, a childsoldier myself, when I swapped my eyes for the killing laser-irises and learnt to inflict the whirling-death on cities. I don't know why I came back."

For a moment the childsoldier seemed to lose his reserve. " You were here once, you the most famous musician in the Dispersal of Man?"

"Is it strange to you that someone can survive the years of child- soldiery?"

"I have never thought of it," the boy said wistfully. "Were you really here? You must be a thousand years old."

Sajit smiled a little at this. "Almost."

"Why did you come back?"

Idly Sajit touched his old whisperlyre; the strings stole warmth from

his fingers, adding it to their resonance. He looked at the room they had given him behind the small stage that was used for the childsoldiers' assemblies, for making announce-ments, for meting out punishments.

It seemed little different from the grubby rooms of his childhood: first as a whore's son in Airang, then here in the childsoldiers' city, impressed by the Inquest into the trade of killing. He wished he had not come back. From the minute he had set foot on Bellares, the barrack world, he wanted to go back to Elloran's palace, to be again among beautiful things.

"I asked for a leave of absence from my Inquestor," he told the boy, "so that I could better remember certain flavors, certain smells, certain colors. I am writing a new music for him, you see." But now that he had seen he did not think he wanted to remember these things. He had not expected the years to have softened the past's ugliness so much. He wished he could tell the boy about Varezhdur the golden palace that flew from star to star through the light-mad overcosm; of the gardens within labyrinthine gardens, of the long dark corridors lined with holosculptures of weeping pteratygers that slowly flapped their wings in the wuthering artwind. But it was useless to talk of such things. Doubtless the boy would be dead in a year. Instead, he simply said, "Over there, the amplijewels — hand them to me. Here. And the belt with the buckle of mating flamefish. And . . . what is your name, boy? You've attended me three days and I'm tired of calling you hey, boy."

"N-narop," said the boy. Then, bursting out, "You asked my name! They never ask me my name." He looked away, embarrassed.

Sajit was dressed now. He gestured for the hover-cushion to descend towards the floor; the boy Narop made to lead him by the hand. Sajit said,

"No, no. I'm really not a thousand years old, you know." The boy shrank away, afraid of offending. For Sajit came as Inquestral envoy, and a word from him could mean instant death, just like that. Sajit knew this too well.

Things weren't that different after all.

A displacement plate was set into the floor; Sajit saw a small insect crawl onto it and vanish. As he made to step out of the room he saw the boy, anxious, unsure. He beckoned him forward. I was like this once, he thought. He tried to drown out the memory in the strains of the music he was about to perform; but it kept surfacing. "What did you mean, Narop-without-a-clan," he said, "when you said you wanted to be a comet when you die?"

"You know, a comet."

"A comet comet?"

"Yes. An angel of death. You know. They build them here. I think they'll show you the factories so you can report to your Inquestor."

"Comet? Angel of death? Some new weapon then?" For he remembered no such thing, and he had thought the boy meant some pretty conceit, some childish daydream.

The boy said, smiling ingenuously, "Maybe they didn't have them in your time, Shen Sajit. But we all dream about them. If we are fierce in battle, if we are unwavering in our loyalty, they reward us after we die by making us into comets. I thought it was something they always had."

"Where is the factory?"

"By the hospice, where they take the childsoldiers to die. It all makes sense." For a moment his citrine eyes glowed like hollow fire, and Sajit was afraid. He knew that a glance and a subvocalized command was all that the boy needed to slice him in two, more cleanly than any knife. If done well there wouldn't even be much blood; the burn's intensity would cauterize the vessels. . . .

The words of the song, Sajit thought. The homeworld of the heart ... the homeworld of the heart. . . . But somehow his heart wasn't in it. His mind saw vivid nightmares of war: of ships burning as they struck the atmosphere of a doomed world, of dismembered children littering the steelgray of a starship's hold. These things had all been real, real as the gold that burnished the palace of Elloran the High Inquestor; to the boy Narop they must be the only reality.

Impulsively he said, "Have you thought about . . . beyond the wars? The time after, if you survive?"

"No, Shen Sajit. I'm afraid to think such things. I don't want a clan name. I want the tumblejoy. They say that a comet feels it, that it's the finest feeling you can have."

"When they take me to see the comets, Narop-without-a-Clan," Sajit said, "will you attend me?"

The boy nodded. And the old musician clutched the whisperlyre to his chest, gasping at the sudden chill as his body heat funnelled into it and fueled its whispering resonances, and he stepped onto the plate, his eyes closed; and as he opened them he saw the clashing lights and heard the familiar murmur-roar of the crowd, and his voice came to him at last, as he knew it would.

***

They had cheered him, worshipped him; now the performance was over, and Narop had escorted him to his quarters, and he had slept fitfully; and when he awoke the word comet was on his lips. For he had dreamt of an army of childsoldiers turned comets and given the power to soar the night skies of a doomed world.

As he sat up and the floor contoured itself to support him, he felt strangely old. Once he and Ton Elloran, the Inquestor he served, had been boys together, friends even; now Sajit was aging while Elloran had not even begun to feel the touch of time. And when I am gone, he thought, he will go on and on, and he will forget me, because there is so much else that he must do. He must play the great game of makrugh, make war and peace with the other Inquestors. Sajit knew the doctrine by heart: man, a fallen being, needed wars to prevent stagnation, to prevent the heresy of utopia. But the Inquest, in its compassion, had taken all the guilt of war upon itself; and now not the shortlived but the Inquestors, with their games, decided the lives and deaths of star systems, and sent out the childsoldiers to kill. And because they bore all the guilt, and the guilt was more than men could bear (for though they ruled the million worlds of the Dispersal of Man, yet they were still no more than men), they had refined the game of makrugh, they had imbued it with artistry, they had made it beautiful. Even Sajit himself was not without guilt, living as he did in the shadow of the High Inquest; his music was much in demand as an exquisite backdrop to some of the bloodiest makrughs ever played.

That was why he had come to Bellares: not to escape the beautiful, but to understand the ugly. For one gave rise to the other, and they were inextricably woven in the tapestry of birth and death.

He heard breathing behind him. He turned. It was Narop, the child- soldier he had talked to before, and a woman he had not yet met. She wore a robe stitched from the skins of a dozen species of snakes. He recognized it as a sign of the Clan of Aush, whose special province was the linking of art and war.

"I am Aush Keshmin," she said. The voice; low, breathy; she could have been a musician, Sajit thought, evaluating it automatically. "Your childsoldier-in-attendance tells me that you have expressed an interest in our comets. I'm flattered, naturally, that an artist of your stature should throw a passing glance at our fledgling military art. As director of the comet project, I have had the honor of being involved in every stage of the design. . . ."

"I told him I wanted to be one when I die," Narop said eagerly.

Keshmin silenced him with a quick glance. He cowered for a moment, and then stood sharply to attention. "That day will come sooner than you want," Keshmin said, "if you don't learn to quell your impertinence!"

Then she turned to Sajit, all smiles.

Sajit watched the boy. He was stiff as a statue now. Only a slight quiver of the lip revealed his terror. "Leave the boy be," he said to the woman.

She said, "As you wish, Shen Sajit. But you cannot be too hard on the creatures. They are not bred for compassion, like you people from the fancy courts of Inquestors. We drain the pity from them the day they first come here."

"I know, Aush Keshmin," Sajit said. "I know."

The military artist looked at him curiously for a moment. He said, "I have been here before."

"I see." She would not meet his eyes now, but shied away from him as if he were tainted.

"Perhaps, Keshmin, you will guide me now?" Sajit was buckling his kaleidokilt now, leaning his arm on Narop's shoulder. "I want so much tolearn what it is you do. My Inquestor will want to know everything."

"Undoubtedly he already does, for it was from his palace that the conceit originated; the comet as death-angel."

"My master no longer plays makrugh," Sajit said. "It must be some other Inquestor." And already, in his mind, he was wondering who it could be: was it Siriss of the white hair and opal eyes, or cruel-mouthed Ton Satymyrys, who thought only of arcane pleasures, or Karakad, the masked Inquestor, whose face no man had seen in a hundred years? These and many more met in the gardens of Elloran's palace to play the deadly game.

"Be that as it may," Aush Keshmin said, "come now." She began walking towards the only displacement plate in the small room. Sajit had the distinct impression that she was hiding something, some inner sadness. He did not think that she would have chosen this field, though one could not argue with the Inquestral granting of a clan-name. It was the only way to escape from being planetbound, from being a peasant, from meeting a childsoldierly death.

***

He followed her down straight gray corridors that cut across each other at right angles. He could not tell them apart, except that some had holosculptures of starships poised for attack, or companies of childsoldiers with the cloaks flying and the killing light streaming from their pitiless eyes. Some corridors were so long that Sajit could see no end to them, for the walls seemed to converge into distant pinpricks of light. They said nothing for a while; the boy was rigid, fearful of being rebuked again, while the woman's face was set into a mask, revealing nothing.

Finally, Sajit asked, "Are we below ground or above it?"

The woman laughed. "What does it matter, Shen Sajit? You are in hell. That's what matters. Tell that to your Inquestors."

But presently they reached an airchute, and Sajit followed the soldier and the artist as they jumped into it and floated upward. The walls became less gray, almost translucent; finally they were completely deopaqued, and Sajit saw that they were in the sunlight over a chessboard landscape, fields walled with barbed wire, cities of steel whose towers knifed the violet sky.

A floater awaited them, and in a moment they were slicing through the planet's dense, fragrant air. Sajit looked out over the fields, and he saw sights from his childhood. Here a batallion of childsoldiers on hoverdisks whirled in unison, the killing light darting from their eyes, kindling distant targets and toppling tall towers of a pseudocity. Even from this height he could hear the shrill warcry : Isha ha! Isha ha! It was a sound all humankind feared, a pure sound, pitiless, yet strangely innocent, for how these children truly know what it was they did? They whirled over the fields like locusts. Sajit ached, knowing how narrowly he himself had missed the final tumblejoy.

And presently they came to a starport that haunched out over a hill; and they took a shuttleglobe out beyond Bellares's atmosphere. And in all this time, since her bitter outburst, Keshmin had not said a word; the boy was frozen in a posture of attention; and Sajit stood watching the sky as it shifted imperceptibly from violet to dark blue to starry black. At last he saw where they were headed: a hospice, a vessel of bubbles and spikes, growing in the distance. Such places, he remembered, were often beyond the atmosphere, for some battlewounds were best treated without the encumbrance of gravity.

Suddenly Narop cried out; the woman did not chide him. He pointed up. Sajit looked. Beyond the hospice, three comets arced, one over the other, their tails twining in a braid of light.

He looked from boy to woman. Keshmin looked uneasy, as if fearful of his reaaion. "It's breathtaking," he said at last, and for the first time she smiled, and he could see a certain beauty behind the stern lips, the care-sunken cheeks.

"I designed them," said Aush Keshmin.

And the boy repeated, "When I die, hokh'Shen, that's where I'm going."

***

Inside the hospice, Sajit was led into an atrium upon which the stars shone through a deopaquement of its domed high ceiling. Two fountains, fire and water, played on either side of them; it was all very restful. A crying, like a birdchoir in the dawn, pervaded the huge chamber. It came from the tier upon tier of levels that opened onto the atrium. The hall was so vast that the levels seemed like shelves, and the beds of dying children like boxes of toy soldiers; it was because it came from so f^ar away, and from all sides, that their deathcrying was transmuted into the singing of birds. When Sajit looked up, he saw the three comets dance through the skywall.

"When they are about to die," Keshmin said, "we bring them here, we set up their deathbeds under the cometlight ... it seems to ease their pain. Will you visit with our dying?"

Sajit nodded. Already he wanted to leave, to return to the palace; but there was something about this woman.

With every look she taunted him. He followed her; the childsoldier walked behind, each step the perfect regulation length. A displacement plate took them up to one of the floors; in pallets against the walls, as far as he could see, the children lay dying.

He followed as Keshmin went among them, whispering a word to one, holding the hand of another.

"Yes," she would say, replying to a hoarse question, "yes, you've been very loyal, they will choose you, I'm sure, they will, they will; you'll be up there in the sky, zooming and zinging among the stars." The words seemed to come automatically to her, a ritual formula.

She was saying it for the fourth or fifth time when the child whose hand she was holding actually started to die. Sajit saw her, a pitiful rag of a little girl . . . how old could she have been? Seven? Eight? As he watched, the girl's eyelids began to flutter uncontrollably, and colors shifted on the holoscreen where a monitoring thinkhive was displaying her vital data. Aush Keshmin seemed to be listening to something, then to issue a subvocalized command with a flick of her mind.

All at once, a forceglobe formed about the dying child's head, abruptly severing it. As Sajit stared, dumbstruck by the sudden horror, the globe floated upward to a displacement plate in the ceiling. The eyelids were still fluttering, the mouth half opened in a silent scream. Sajit looked down at the headless corpse; a hundred metal tendrils had slithered into place about the neckstump, cauterizing, sucking away the blood.

"What does this mean?" he shouted. His voice echoed about the four walls of the great atrium. "What have you done to the child?"

Aush Keshmin's voice was distant, cold: "Don't shout, Shen Sajit; you'll disturb the others. Tonight we will see the girl dancing in the starlight. We're talking about a new kind of weapon, you know. A weapon that feels rage and wants vengenance, a weapon with a soul. That's what our comets have, you see! Better to serve the mysterious purposes of the High Inquest . . ."

"But the girl — "

"Her brain. Master Musician. It has to be fresh if it is to be at the center of the comet's consciousness. . . ."

Sajit looked from the woman to the childsoldier Narop. Through the hall the deathsighs of a thousand children echoed, like windchimes, like the tuning-up of a distant flutechoir. There stood the woman who had designed this twisted artifact. He marveled that she showed so little emotion at a child's death. Perhaps her mind was dulled; perhaps the single death was insignificant beside what that death could inflict, the death of millions more. "Do you feel no compassion, then?" he said.

"Compassion, Shen Sajit? That's for Inquestors to feel. My duty is to my art."

"A cold, bleak art."

"But there is beauty in it, musician, a grace of heartache in the slow arc of death."

"Show me more, then. I must see it all." The woman frightened him more and more. When he'd been a childsoldier, though, so long ago, he had thought he could fear nothing. She is so desolate, he thought, so hopeless, and yet she still believes herself an artist. What if I had been commanded by the Inquest to be a maker of toys of death? Could I still live with myself?

Aush Keshmin said, "You will see all, of course. That is your privilege as Inquestral delegate."

"Yes. Narop, come." He turned to look for the boy.

Narop was standing at the very edge of the tier. His gaze was fixed on the deopaqued ceiling and the starstream.

The three comets had shifted now. They were chasing each other, their tails radiating out in a Catherine wheel, blurring. Now the comets broke loose from their tight circle and they began to soar and dive like porpoises in a sea of night. Now they flew in formation, tails swerving in concert.

The child stared at them with such terrible yearning ... it was this longing that frightened Sajit most of all. For a moment he had recognized it in himself, but had dismissed the thought, had buried it in a mass of irrelevances, for he could not bear to admit the longing to himself.

And now they were in a starship and leaving Bellares behind. It was beautiful, this planet of killing children, when seen from afar, Sajit thought, as he watched the patterned lightstreaks crisscrossing the planet's mistlayer, bluewhite and fringed with violet where the sun's diamond peered through it. The woman Keshmin never met his eyes, but stared outwards, through the deopaqued screens that showed the three comets. Behind them were delphinoid warships.

"What is this?" he said. "You're taking me to a war, woman?"

"And why not? You demanded to be shown everything. Look at the comets. Soon we'll leave Bellares behind. As the sunlight fades, so will their streams of luminescent almost-vacuum. Soon they'll be dark and cold, like the hearts of the Inquestors that cause the wars to happen."

Sajit listened in silence, awed by the image. She went on, still avoiding his eyes: "But they won't be as cold as those mindless chunks of ice that orbit every star . . . each one has a precision thinkhive that controls its every movement, and each one is animated by a vengeful spirit . . . the brain of a dying childsoldier!"

"They are alive, then."

"Alive and not alive, master musician," said the military artist. "They're in a state of half-awareness, a kind of hypnosis, perhaps. These are brains that burn with loyalty to the Inquest. They see and hear through powerful prosthetics. They speak to us only when we give them machines to speak through. Soon the thinkhives will forge a dark corridor through the tachyon universe, and we will be in the vicinity of the world to be destroyed; the comets will catch fire from the sunlight and will dance their doomsayings over the chief cities of the world that is to fall beyond; then, at my signal, their dance will reach fever pitch, and they will fall upon the cities and crush them. It is beautiful, isn't it?"

Sajit said, "What is the world?"

"It is called Korith."

"Why will it *fall beyond?*"

"That I don't know. It's the will of the Inquest, of course, and in their compassion they have arranged for the people bins to carry off most of the population. We don't question the Inquest, Shen Sajit; we're soldiers. Come, do you wish to see more?"

They flicked by displacement plate into another chamber. There were strange instruments here, and forcecases that held human brains linked by wires to control panels. The walls were all deopaqued, so that it seemed that they rested on a platform drifting through empty space; and above their heads the comets swam still, their tails dim now.

"Why are we here?" Sajit asked.

"The control room," Keshmin said. And she summoned a hoverchair and was soon bent over some controls, while Sajit stared at the brains that hung in the air, forcebubbled, quivering a little. "Look!" As Sajit looked around him, at the spearal starscape, he saw the stars shimmer strangely; he felt a queasy, dead sensation crawling up his throat from his stomach. He knew then that they were preparing to break open a tachyon corridor, to breach the space between spaces. For this was war, and war must be fought instantaneously; it could not wait for the leisurely pace of pinhol- ing through the overcosm. As he watched, a wedge of blackness parted the starstream and grew wider and wider, as though the sky was a skin and, the darkness a surgical incision held open by forceps; and they were accelerating towards the cleft. . . .

And abruptly, it closed behind them, and they were in another region of space; for now the band of the starstream stretched up and down, and a red star dangled from it like a cherry.

"The Korith system?" said Sajit.

"Yes," said Keshmin.

As she spoke, the three comets soared into existence overhead, having made the crossing in the starship's field. Sajit saw other delphinoid ships too: full, he knew, of childsoldiers. A pearl of a planet ballooned abruptly out of the dark. "Korith?" said Sajit.

"Yes. And now the dance will begin."

The comets were one, three- tailed now, arrow-aimed at the half- world. Awed, Sajit watched. Now the tails broke free of the strand and they whirled, blinding-fast, like a Catherine wheel. Now the three separated, swam like flamefish through the black. Now they arched as one, now three, now one, now three . . .

"They will be seeing them now, on Korith," said Keshmin. A grim smile stole over her features. Sajit watched first the woman, then the boy, whose eyes shone with longing. He thought; I have never hated the universe so much.

"What are you thinking, master singer?" Keshmin said. "You don't have to tell me. You think I'm tainted, don't you? You despise me." "How can you call this art?"

"And you, hokh 'Shen! What about you? It's you who lull the Inquestors' minds after they have decreed these world-burnings, isn't it? It's you who envelop your masters with beauty, so they no longer understand about death that falls without reason from the sky."

"No!" Sajit trembled. This was a sorry woman, a vicious, callous woman . . . how was it then that her words rang true? He turned away. "Give me a private chamber. I will not watch this war. I'm going to compose. Attend me, boy."

"Coward!" Aush Keshmin hissed after him, as his feet sought the displacement plate.
***

Narop led him to a spartan square chamber walled with metalfrost. He sank down onto the yielding floor. There was a whisperlyre there, and a starharp of concert size, the seven frames of strings fanning out from the controlseat like a silvery asterisk. The grayness of the room rested his eyes. The boy stood guard.

Presently he said: "What do you think of all this, then, Narop-without-a-Clan?"

"That your kind, master, are too delicate for war."

"Delicate! Delicate!" Sajit shouted. "No, don't be afraid, don't shy away like that. Shall I. sing you a song of space battles, of heroism and courage?"

"If you wish, hokh'Shen . " And the boy settled back against the dull wall to listen.

Sajit performed, as much for himself as for the boy. But the words of the songs seemed empty. Presently curiosity overcame him; he thought of the three comets and their cold stardance. He ordered the walls deopaqued so he could see them. Once more the night engulfed them, and they saw the comets: writhing, twisting, zigzagging over the darkside of the crescent planet.

And behind the world, a fleet of delphinoid ships, waiting to rain destruction. Like a swarm of phosphorflies.

Then came an alarm. A metallic screech, earsplitting. "What is the matter?"

A voice: Alert. Alert. Stations. Stations. "What is the matter now?" The alarm awoke old memories in Sajit, memories he had thought buried forever. Once, once only, he had escaped a shredded starship —

"Come, boy," he said. The boy — he could see that the boy was clenching back terror — preceded him to the displacement plate. They stepped into the control room of wires and floating brains —

"What has happened?" Sajit cried. "I am an Inquestral ambassador.

Are we being attacked?"

He saw Aush Keshmin now, white. Her lips hardly moved. She pointed at the deopaqued ceiling.

A comet had broken loose, disrupting the pattern. It was making its way towards the fleet.

"It has awakened," she said. "Malfunction of its lifesupport ... it has decided to attack us!"

"Why?" Sajit whispered.

"It was a terrible idea. To give them consciousness. There was always the possibility. It's gone mad, Shen Sajit, mad!"

"Retreat, then! Abort the mission."

"And the other comets? Their programming is set. The Inquest will not be pleased."

"How long do you have?" >

"A few hours yet, hokh'Shen . "

"Hours . . ."

Aush Keshmin played with control panels. Lights darted across holo- screens. "I am opening a communicating channel," she said, "switching on the comet's eyes and ears so we can hear its thoughts . . . now."

And then Sajit could hear it, a faint, kittenlike voice, like the edge of a wind —

Ma . . . ma

"What does this mean?" he cried.

Ma . . . ma

"By all the powers of powers !" Aush Keshmin said. "The child was not quite dead enough. It has woken from its trance state. It's afraid. It's found something it doesn't like. But that's impossible! We selea the children for the utmost loyalty to the Inquest. They are screened, tested, psychically probed to the limit — "

"But what is it saying?"

"Why, it's crying for its mother, of course. Childsoldiers often do that, the first day or two of training."

Sajit hated her then. He knew that the woman cared only for the chill beauty of her deathdance, and not at all that a child was in pain. He tried to remember the pain himself. He saw himself fleeing down the flametwisted corridors of a dying starship. For a fleeting moment it was more real to him than all the splendor of Elloran's Varezhdur.

And the woman was saying, "We will have to destroy them all."

But Sajit said, "Will you not find out what kind of child this was? Its name? Its former homeworld? Perhaps there will be some information you can use."

"Very well," said Keshmin stonily.

Ma . . . ma

Sajit remembered the voice now. His own past. Once he had had a mother. How long ago? Time dilations had taken their toll, and she must be lost in the far past.

Keshmin was subvocalizing instructions to the central thinkhive of the ship now. For a while they heard nothing but the whining of the little lost voice. Then came the thinkhive's voice, metallic, echoey : The comet that is now insane, Aush Keshmin, was once Yryan-without-a-Clan, son of a merchant of Korith —

"You fool!" shouted Sajit. "You sent a childsoldier against his own home world! In my day such a thing was never done!"

"You don't understand! That's no child out there, it's a machine, malfunctioning ..."

Out of the silence came the childish voice: *Mama . . . bad men are coming . . . they want to kill you . . . but I'll stop them . . . stop them . . .*

"I will communicate with it," Aush Keshmin said. "Listen, child of the tumblejoy! Resume your programming at once! Or you will be destroyed!" She spoke these words to the air; communicators were relaying them into the mind of the comet.

It's trying to tell me to kill you, mama , . . it's bad, bad, bad, I won't listen . . .

"It's useless to reason with it!"

For a while they stood, master musician and artist of death, hating each other. Finally, Sajit said: "You cannot make it understand, Keshmin, that its mother is long long dead. How can you make it understand? You yourself cannot understand. It fears you. You are evil to it. No, *I* must go to it, Aush Keshmin, because though I

seem now almost as high as the Inquestors, I was once
like this Yryan."

"It is safer to destroy the comets and return,"
Keshmin said sullenly.

"I am an Inquestral ambassador, and I demand to
visit the comet. We still have time. Through Ton
Elloran n'Taanyel Tath, my master, I assume
responsibility."

"You meddling street singer! You'll use this, no
doubt, for one of your melodramatic songs, to ease the
stomachs of Inquestors at dinner parties."

"Say what you want. I have the authority."

Why did I say that now? he thought. What
masochism is it that impels me to pursue the ugly, the
anguished? But I must go. It's my past that calls me.
Ghosts must be faced and exorcised.

Aush Keshmin turned to summon a shuttlecraft.

The pearl-world wheeled above them, ravishing,
doomed.

They did not speak; their anger walled them from
each other. But from across the silence of space, the
comet cried for its mother.

   ***

. . . space now. A shuttlecraft. The comet's tail rearing
up, dividing the night with its swath of radiance.

At first Sajit had insisted on going up to the comet
alone. But it was true that he needed Keshmin's
technical aid; and he wanted the childsoldier there too.
He had an overpowering desire to strip away the boy's
illusions, to show him the degradation behind the
dream. He did not know why he had this urge. It was
almost criminal to open the boy's eyes, to let him see
the utter hopelessness of the universe. Sajit was angry
and bitter.

Presently the band of incandescence filled the whole screen. It was a million klomets long, this dust-tail, and thinner than most vacua; and yet it glowed. When they entered the tail the darkness barely changed; only before and after, in the plane of their flight, was a barely perceptible shining. And in the distance, the head: a snowball of frozen gases with a child's soul at its kernel.

And all the while, as they were approaching, the craft's thinkhive relayed the crying of the comet.

"How much time?"

"Two hours. Then, whether you will or no," said Keshmin, "ambassador or not, you will die, because I have ordered the comets aborted. Do you understand? I obey instructions, Shen Sajit. I do not have whims, as you palace parasites do. Your whim may kill the three of us."

"Quiet! Think of the planet's millions. They will die too."

"We saved as many as we could. Already the people bins have left with as many stasis-packed humans as could be persuaded to leave, threading the overcosm like a million segments of silver centipede."

Grimly, Sajit looked ahead. He clutched his whisperlyre to his chest; at the last moment he had brought it from his room on the starship, needing a sense of security.

They landed. A forcetube dug its way out of the snow. They put on pressure skins; Sajit felt the strange isolation as the unicellular skin warped around his body and his whisperlyre. They plated from the craft; Sajit felt the gutwrench of near-weightlessness. Ahead was the tube of nothing. They walked to it over the icerock peppered with methane snow. Though the pressure skin shielded him from the cold and fed him oxygen, Sajit felt another kind of chill. It was the silence between the stars, the utter aloneness. Once starpilots had sailed this silence, and known nothing of the overcosm.

In moments the three were following the forcetunnel deep into the heart of the comethead. There was a little cell there, lined with instru- ments and walled with gray metal. "Can he see us?" said Sajit. For now that they were at the seat of the comet's soul, they could no longer hear its projected voice.

"Not yet." Keshmin touched a stud; all at once the child's sobbing burst into the chamber. "After I subvoke a few commands to the think- hive, you will become visible to it."

"Stay out of its line of vision," Sajit whispered. He dared not raise his voice. There was a presence here, a thing undead.

Woman and boy stepped into the shadows. He felt their eyes on him, but tried to forget. To concentrate. In front of him were semiorganic machines, spirals and corkscrews of metal fanning out from growths of lichen; and a circlet of mirror metal. His own face stared back at him.

"Make him see me," he whispered. And he called the dead boy's child-name: "Yrieh, Yrieh."

A swirl of mist in the mirror; then a holosculpt image of the boy's face, culled by the thinkhive from its repertory of remembrances . . . eyes of burning amber . . . thin pale lips ... a mane of midnight hair ... he could have been the twin of Narop-without-a-Clan. "Listen, listen, Yrieh. Can you hear me? Can you see me?"

The boy's voice, echobent, tinged with metal: *Who are you? . . . Are you my mother?*

"A friend."

You're from the bad people. I'mnot turning back. I'm going to kill you all, all, all.

"It must be destroyed!" Keshmin whispered urgently.

"Be quiet! Don't let him hear you," said Sajit. To the boy: "I am Sajitteh."

. . . one of the childsoldiers?

"One of the childsoldiers."

Tears streamed down the cheeks of the ghostface in the mirror. *I woke up . . . they tell me I'm dead . . . I'm not dead . . . I'm awake . . . I've got power, kill-power . . . bring me my mother . . . or I'll kill the whole fleet. I'll kill, kill, kill . . .*

"Why, Yrieh, why?" Sajit said. He could hardly contain his anger. "You can tell me."

You'll understand? . . . not like the others.

"You must make him turn around. Or put him back to sleep," Keshmin said, "so that the comet can be operated automatically."

. . . Whose voice? One of them?

"No, Yrieh," said Sajit. "Listen. Your mother's gone, child."

No!

"Are you afraid?"

Yes. Afraid. I woke up in the dark. In the dark, falling towards my homeworld.

"You didn't feel the tumblejoy?"

Joy? Joy?

"The wild joy of the dance of killing? Surely they taught you that?"

Joy? I feel alone, alone, and cold, cold, afraid, afraid.

"Go to sleep."

No! Then I'll never wake up again.

How could he deny that? Never had Sajit felt so angry about the cruelty that the Inquest inflicted so casually, every second of its existence, in the name of the High

Compassion. Sajit searched his mind for a solution. Either alternative meant death for some. Both were death for the child-comet, a second death. Should I lie to him? he thought. Tell him his mother's coming to him?

He pulled out his whisperlyre from his tunic. "I will sing to you," he said. "Then you won't be afraid anymore." And he played a few notes, feeling the lyre suck the warmth from his chest, hearing the plucked sounds echo.

The spectral eyes watched him, wide with innocence. He reminded himself that those eyes had killed. As, once, his own had.

He sang a lullaby. Once his mother had sung it to him. But that was in another time, and could not be brought back.

He sang:
Sleep, child, sleep;
The Inquestors are watching you
from their far heaven.
The wings of pteratygers are fanning you '.
The war is done.
Your mother's arms are warm.
Sleep, child, sleep.

As Sajit sang he began to weep. He could not help himself. Often he had wept in concerts; this was part of his art, something that moved audiences, that could be controlled. Not this. He wept for his own lost childhood. He wept for his Inquestor, Elloran, who had drowned himself in beauty so that he might not feel the pain. As he sang the whisperlyre stole all his body heat, compounding its resonance with it. He was so cold.

But still he sang:
The war is done.

Your mother 's arms are warm.
Sleep, child, sleep.
And the wraithface in the mirror closed its eyes and was beautiful in sleep, and at peace.

Sajit said, "I have taken away his pain. That is my art."

He turned to his two companions. Aush Keshmin was shaking, nervous; she could not meet his eyes. He seized her by the chin and forced her to look at him. "Now, death-artist! Do you see what you've done? You turn children into monsters, but in their hearts they have not lost their innocence utterly. They are not beasts."

Keshmin said, "I didn't know that before. No. I did know. But I buried what I knew. I knew that any clan-name was better than none. Please, master musician, take my name from me."

"The comet will function properly now?"

"Yes. It will fall on Korith and destroy cities."

"And do you rejoice?"

"How can I?"

And then Sajit turned to the boy Narop. He stood in the wall's shadow, shuffling his feet. "Look at me, Narop!" Sajit cried. "Is this what you want to be when you die?"

And suddenly, appallingly, the boy began to cry. He was only a little boy after all. Sajit saw the crumpled sable cloak and the iridium boots, too shiny, and knew them to be toy armor for toy soldiers . . . "Don't cry," he said tenderly. To the woman he said, "Don't despair." And to both: "Where there is bitterness there must be beauty too. It has always been so, and always will be. I will free you."

For he knew now why he had been moved to come to Bellares, to the place of his tormented childhood ... it was as the woman had put it. To make a song to ease the stomachs of Inquestors, she had said. That was true, but not the whole truth.

They returned to the craft, and thence to the starship. Sajit did not choose to watch the end of the dance of comets, nor the death of Korith. He had seen such things before. He knew what he would see from far in space; a sudden vaporous burning in the planet's atmosphere, a patch or two of brilliance ... an eruption of diamonds on the surface . . . and the chain of people bins, spiralling into space like a necklace, seeking an entrance to the overcosm where they would sail the centuries until another world was found for them.

But when he left for Varezhdur, he took Keshmin and Narop with him. And they were with him when he was ushered at last into the throneroom of Ton Elloran, his master, whom trillions called the compassionate one.

The gold, the gold . . .

They passed through hallways with gilt-bumished walls, inlaid with highscript poems in lapis lazuli, Sajit's own poems . . . groves of gcld- plated arbors crisscrossed with streams that glittered with gold dust . . . the woman gaped, sullen at first, uncomprehending . . . the childsoldier cried out in delight . . . and Sajit saw that they had reached the corridor lined with a hundred reliefed ptertygers of Ontian marble, and he knew that he was home. And in a moment they were in Elloran's throneroom, built around Dei Zhendra's great galaxy of dust. A shimmerviol music played from a hidden alcove, and the chill pure voice of a neuterchild was singing one of Sajit's own songs.

Sajit looked at his master, who sat, closed-eyed, on a great throne.

"Elloran," he said.

Abruptly, the music stopped.

Elloran opened his eyes. How old he was! Had Sajit been gone that long, then? "Elloran, I'm home."

"Who are these?"

"The woman was once a maker of deathtoys. The boy was once a childsoldier. But Elloran, they are not what they were made to be! They have poetry in them." Sajit came closer to the throne. He saw his master'sface: how tired, how world-weary. The shimmercloak itself dwarfed him, and the huge throne of gold. And he beckoned Aush Keshmin and Narop-without-a-Clan to him, but they cowered behind him, not daring to stare at the throne's brilliance.

"Oh, Sajitteh, Sajitteh," Elloran said, "always the redeemer! You'd save the souls of everyone in the universe, if you could."

"And what of it?" Sajit said, his anger bursting out at last. And he told Elloran what he had seen. How they'd been making dead children into deathweapons. How one had awakened in terror and gone mad. And how he had lulled it to sleep with an ancient song, and given it an illusion of peace. "Why do you let these things happen, Elloran?" he cried out.

"Tell me, Sajit. Were they not beautiful, these comets, when they danced?"

"Yes. That was the most terrible thing."

"Is there not pain in everything beautiful . . . ? It is true that I let this happen. But once, long ago, at a game of makrugh, you were singing us a new song as we played at burning worlds. Do you remember the words? Perhaps not. You have written a thousand songs. Here, though, are lines from the song:

What if the stars had life?
What if the comets felt anger
As they burned across the space between worlds?

"It was your song, Sajit, that gave rise to the idea — "

"No!" cried Sajit. "It was your players of makrugh who twisted my meaning into a cruel conceit!"

"Sajitteh. . . ." Sajit saw terrible sadness in the Inquestor's eyes. And because he loved his master, he could not be angry.

"I know," he said, "that you too are trapped by the Inquest's doctrine. You are compelled to maintain the stasis of the Dispersal of Man, and to create such little wars as may be necessary to give the illusion of movement; it is thus that you preserve the balance between utopianism and progress."

"You could almost be an Inquestor," said Elloran, jesting to hide the hurt.

"You don't fool me. You too are a victim, imprisoned by your own power."

"Yes. Yes."

"That, Elloran, is the lesson I learnt on Bellares, and at the comet's heart."

"And what else did you learn?"

"That we must wrest from the universe every fleeting moment of beauty, of freedom, of truth."

"Old lessons, Sajitteh." Elloran closed his eyes again.

Sajit said to his two companions: "You are free now. Elloran has released you. You can stay in Varezhdur and travel through Elloran's worlds; or you can leave. You will be given money. What do you want?"

Keshmin said, "It's so beautiful here ... I didn't know . . ."

"Can I serve you?" said Narop. "I'll be your slave."

"I am a slave," said Sajit. The thought no longer rankled him. "By all means, then, stay. Drink in Varezhdur's loveliness. When the time comes, you will want to leave, like I did, and face the ugliness again; and perhaps you will want to return. But for now, be happy."

He summoned an usher to find them apartments in the palace. Keshmin smiled at last. The boy was walking on air as they left.

Finally he was alone with Ton Elloran n'Taanyel Tath, Lord of Varezhdur, Princeling of Many Tributaries.

"Well, Sajitteh!" said Ton Elloran. "Two saved. How many more to go?"

Sajit didn't answer; he only smiled. Then he said, "How long was I gone?"

"Forever. It must have been only a few years to you; for me it was a century."

"No wonder you seem old."

"Old! I missed you, Sajitteh." His eyes sparkled. "What was that lullaby you sang to the child-comet?"

"A silly ditty, Inquestor, quite without art. My mother sang it to me once."

"Sing it to me."

"But —"

"Come, Sajitteh! Only chance has elevated me above that child whose soul they planted in a comet. That's why I need you. To remind me that I'm still human. I am, you know. Human. Yes. I, the all-wise, the all-compassionate . . . the burner of worlds."

Sajit sang. Without an instrument, in a soft comforting voice. Just the way he remembered it from childhood, before they took him away to Bellares, to be a childsoldier.

As he sang he watched the Inquestor's face. What worries plagued him now? What problems of planets? He could not tell. But he meant to soothe the pain. That was his art. Illusion, perhaps, but still art.

Elloran slept.

Somtow performs a wedding (from HELLO magazine)

Despatches from Earth
His Beatitude Performs a Wedding

Last week I did something I haven't done for thirty years — I presided over a wedding in my capacity as a Universal Life Church Minister. This was a family affair — my niece was marrying a notoriously outspoken journalist. It was truly the union of fire and ice, as I pointed out in my remarks.

There was a fair amount of High Society — ex-prime ministers, ambassadors, and social media influencers present, as well as *HELLO* magazine, who suggested I should perform more weddings. They even offered to get me clients.

Well, everyone said I ought to publish my sermon, so here goes....

THE PREAMBLE

Today I'm appearing in a rôle most of you have never seen me play — I'm solemnizing a wedding. It is, indeed, the wedding of the century. The union of fire and ice, the proverbial collision between the immovable and the unstoppable. It is Meghan and Harry, Jon Snow and Danaerys Targaryen, perhaps even Lucifer and Jesus — though I'd leave you to figure out which is which.

To what do I owe this privilege? What have I done to merit the honour of presiding over this monumental celebration?

In my sermon, I will be expounding on the mystery that is love, and try to explain how fire and ice can belong together, nay, *should* belong together. I will tell you the story of how fate brought this couple together. But that's for later.

But in this brief introduction, I'll start by answering a question that many may be wondering. What the hell am I doing here?

Well, my friends in Thailand may not realize this, but I am a legally ordained minister of the Universal Life Church. This church, founded in 1959 in Modesto, California, has a single credo: "Do what is right." You too may become legally ordained by this church in about ten seconds, just by going to their website.

Lest you think this is just some California silliness, let me name for you some other ordained ministers of the Universal Life Church that you have heard of.

All four of the Beatles. Lady Gaga. Tom Hanks. Courtney Love. Sir Ian McKellen. Gavin Newsom, Lt Governor of California. Conan O'Brien. Hunter S. Thompson. Stephen Colbert.

Any of these ministers (at least, the ones still living) might have been invited to solemnize this wedding, but as fate would have it, the bride and bridegroom chose me. Perhaps the others weren't picking up the phone.

I've performed a number of weddings in California, mostly for members of the science fiction community, most of whom wanted outlandish elements that no self-respecting mainstream cleric could provide. The Universal Life Church, however, is a very big tent. Eccentrics, Misfits, and Basket Cases are welcome. This is my first time performing such a ceremony for what might be regarded as "respectable" people. It is truly an eye-opener.

I would like to add that though I am licensed to do this in California, Thailand is a little far from Modesto.

Therefore, in order to ensure the legitimacy of today's proceedings, I hereby declare that the spot I am standing on, to a radius of ten meters, will now formally secede from the Kingdom and is now an extraterritorial county of California.

This secession will last until the moment the happy couple are actually married, at which point we shall restore sovereignty to the Kingdom of Thailand.

You are all now officially seeking asylum. Better do it quick, before the wall comes!

With any luck, the junta won't reclaim this territory for at least 30 minutes. If you see them coming, we'll just perform the ceremony faster.

So ... enough about me. Let's talk about *them*. You will soon see them in all their splendour and I will be narrating them epic tale of how *they* met, and how they fit into the grand cycle of the universe.

And here comes the bridesmaids' procession — let the spectacle begin!

***

THE SERMON

About two hundred thousand years ago, according to modern scientists, there lived a woman to whom the DNA of every single person alive today can be traced. She's been given the nickname "Mitochondrial Eve." From this woman sprang the entirety of humanity, in its diversity, its teeming billions, its dreams that have spanned all space and time, its ability to contemplate of infinity and eternity.

The reason all of us here are today is that Mitochondrial Eve met a guy. Ten thousand generations later, her descendants have conquered the world. And thus it is that the story of mankind, and the story of love, are one and the same story.

For these two people to stand before us today, ten thousand generations later, there must have been twenty thousand acts of love. For all of us to be here in this magical moment, there were millions of such acts. For the world, billions.

There is a chain of being, two hundred thousand years long and going through countless acts of love, that leads from Mitochondrial Eve to Vanina and Pravit.

Today, therefore, we celebrate a sacred mystery, older than any recorded history, and as profound and unfathomable today as it was two hundred thousand years ago.

I would like to talk a little bit about this mystery. I want to tell the story of how love led us to this moment.

Since it might go a little bit over my time limit to tell the *whole* story, you'll understand if I leave out a few bits.

So let's jump to ancient Egypt and I want to read to you one of the earliest known texts about love. This is 4000-year-old poem so poorly preserved that some of its hieroglyphics can't be translated.

Your love has penetrated all within me
Like honey plunged into water,
Like an odor which penetrates spices,
As when one mixes juice in ... "indecipherable."

What did I say? It's a mystery.

Perhaps less ambiguous are the words of Sappho, one of the greatest poets of the ancient world. She was so famous that most people could recite her poems from memory — so they didn't keep copies. So written copies were often cut into strips and used as wrappings for mummifying cats.

One cat, when de-mummified, yielded up the following fragment:

As a mountain wind swoops down upon an oak
  Love shook my heart.

The rest of this 2,500 year old poem is missing.

But what we can glean from this fragment is that love is this huge, sweeping thing that no human can resist.

My final excerpt of ancient poetry is from the *Song of Songs,* and it shows you just how difficult it is to describe the one you love:

Your hair is like a flock of goats,
  Your teeth are like a flock of shorn sheep
  Your two breasts are like two fawns ...
  Your belly is a heap of wheat ....

No, that's not a guide to animal husbandry. It's just to show you that explaining why you love someone is an elusive thing. She's like a herd of goats, a pile of wheat. In the same poem she says he's like ivory encrusted with sapphires, like alabaster columns ... apparently permanently hard.

This is what we've gleaned from the wisdom of the ancients: that love can boil down to the indecipherable; that love is a thing of elemental fury that sweeps you away; and that love confounds all metaphors.

Let's skip a few thousand years now, because I'm sure you want me to get the couple at hand. There's plenty of mystery here, no end of elemental fury, and much that beggars description. Let us try.

The news that Pravit and Vanina were to be wed was met with shock, awe, and disbelief by many of their most ardent fans. Yet it is clear evidence of an epic destiny that has worked itself out over the last two hundred thousand years.

My niece Vanina has been called a difficult woman. Certainly, in this culture of strutting, macho males, it's hard to find a man able to cope with a female of her intellect and accomplishments. She's blessed with enormous brain power, steely determination, and a sense of self-assured certitude that has frightened many a man. Holder of three nationalities, she is a citizen of the world, comfortable in any culture. She comes from a long line of powerful women. Believe me, I know this. I've frequently felt their power.

So what kind of a man is Pravit? He's immensely intelligent, and immensely principled. His writings, his strongly held views, his refusal to be bullied by authority figures portend a level of fearlessness that will serve him well in the coming adventure.

From certain online video clips, certain published statements, it seems that the world has surmised that this couple is firmly planted on opposite sides of Thailand's political spectrum. This wedding is already being painted as a battle royale — with comparisons between the marriage of James Carville and Mary Matalin, or Kellyanne and George Conway.

The truth, as always, is a lot more nuanced.

Though I've known Pravit since his childhood, I came to know him better when I decided to invite him to speak at the Oxford-Cambridge dinner two years

ago. I did so not only because I admire his bravery and
outspokenness, but because I wanted to show that our
country and our culture isn't about Manichean
dualities.

Pravit performed this balancing act well, and was
not dragged away by the secret police after his speech.
He also made a profound impression on my mother,
who later opined that here was a man who *could* be
Vanina's intellectual peer. A few days later she called
me and suggested that I should attempt to bring them
together.

I didn't think I could be successful in the
completely unfamiliar role of yenta, but I was willing to
give it a shot.

I arranged a meeting at an all-you-can-eat Brazilian
fogo restaurant, prepared for a pleasant dinner with a
couple of smart people. Nothing prepared me for the
whirlwind that followed.

The dinner ended and the two of them went off for
a glass of wine. I don't know what was in that drink,
but a certain four-thousand-year-old Egyptian poem
comes to mind ... surely the wine contained a hefty
dose of "indecipherable".

The glass of "indecipherable" was followed by
Sappho's swooping mountain wind. This couple was
swept up in a passion so powerful, so all-consuming,
that many predicted it would sputter and go out. It did
not.

Indeed, it was a flame that refused to be spent.
Many opposed the match. Many said unflattering
things. Many predicted disaster. Many ungainly
metaphors were evoked, and not just animal
husbandry. The couple yoyoed between extremes,
from the greatest thing since sliced bread to ultimate
pariahs. But the flame did not go out.

Indeed, their triumph over the tempestuous vicissitudes of their relationship is a living demonstration of another line from the *Song of Songs:* *"Many waters cannot quench love."*

It is customary during the sermon for the officiating cleric to give all sorts of advice to the couple, exhorting them to be good, to love and nurture one another, to be faithful, and so on. Considering the triumphant way they have already overcome so much in order to stand before you today, I find myself with no advice to give that they haven't already handled for themselves.

In the ten thousand generations since Mitochondrial Eve found her man, you stand as worthy recipients of her legacy. With dedication, devotion, and diligence, you will overcome all obstacles and become shining links in the great chain of being that stretches from Eve to the end of the world.

We have come together from all around the world, from every corner of Mitochondrial Eve's diaspora, to share the forging of this link. Let us rejoice in their happiness. Let us celebrate their uniqueness. Let us share their joy, and the love which is driving force of our human journey.

Dearly beloved, it will soon be time to begin the new chapter of the Pravit-Vanina epic.

By tradition, however, I'm required to bring up the escape clause, so here goes: "If any here present knows of any reason why Vanina and Pravit should *not* be married, speak now, or forever hold thy peace."

Any takers? I didn't think so.

So let's get on with it....
***

Now that you have pledged your commitment in front of family and friends, and under the watchful eye of any gods and karmic entities in which you may believe, you will present each other with a visible symbol of that pledge — a ring.

We no longer live in an age where a man must lead and a woman must follow, so I ask that you perform the following ritual together.   Please repeat the following words after me, while placing the ring on the finger of your partner.

> *Our love, like a circle,*
> *has no beginning and no end.*
> *May this ring reside with you always*
> *an outward sign of our souls' commitment.*
> *With this ring I declare*
> *That I am yours, now and forever*
> *In this life and in all my lives to come.*

With the exchange of rings, the ritual is complete.

By the power vested in me by the Universal Life Church and the State of California, I hereby declare Pravit and Vanina to be husband and wife. The deed is done and I formally return the territory we are standing on to the Kingdom of Thailand.

The couple may now kiss.

Congratulations!

Lettercolumn

remarks from our readers...

Write to **inquestortales@bangkokopera.com**

Dear Somtow

please forgive the informal address which comes with my chosen language!

I don't know what you or your family are celebrating at this time of the year, but do hope you have reason and opportunity to get together with friends and family.

Me, I'm celebrating in the Czech Republic with my adoptive family, and I wanted to take the opportunity to thank you for brightening my year with your work, especially the new Inquestor stories. Going back into that universe feels a lot like a warm bath - familiar, comforting, and great to be in. But it also brings the promise of the new, and at the moment I am very much looking forward to the promised exposition of the training and environments which shapes the Child Soldiers !

Besides this I have to say that the additional materials in the chapbooks are a further source of enjoyment, especiallly the initial versions of story fragments, small story arcs, and short stories; even if I'm by no means enough of a superfan to be able to tell with certainty what is Canon or not.

But what really takes the biscuit, so to speak (and in a very positive way, to be clear), are the elaborations on the Inquestral Highspeech by the good Professor Schnau-en-Jip. And, as a student of the Czech language, contending with its sometimes labyrinthine complications, I have to say that it looks like I might be better off wrapping my head around Highspeech instead!

I hope that the new year brings you success, less stress, good health, and lots if time to create the stories and music we so enjoy!

Or, as I'm currently residing in Czechia: *Veselé Vánoce, všechno nejlepší k narozeninám, a štěstí nový rok!*

— Markus Thierstein

— I asked Professor Schnau-en-Jip to reveal a little more about the Highspeech, but he will only release a few pages at a time. In fact, this month he was going to talk some more about the Inquestral verb, but his notes appear to be missing. He's a bit absent minded. You'll have to wait for the next issue.

— Somtow

Dear Somtow,

A lot of the facts about Sajit seem to be different in the new book. I mean not the same as they were in the original IASFM stories. Is this canon?

— It will all be rendered consistent in the end, but I don't want to spoil the surprise.

— Somtow

The Inquestor Series

The Novels

Light on the Sound (1982)
The Throne of Madness (1983)
Utopia Hunters (1984)
The Darkling Wind (1985)

Homeworld of the Heart (in process)
    Part One: *The Singing Moons* (2018)
    Part Two: *A Woman Cloaked in Shadow (2018)*
    Part Three: *The Child Collector (2019)*
    Part Four: *(in process)*

in process
Vara's World

The Short Stories

The Thirteenth Utopia (Analog, 1979)
The Web Dancer (IASFM, 1979)
Darktouch (IASFM, 1980) (non-canonical)
Light on the Sound (IASFM, 1980)
The Rainbow King (IASFM, 1981)
The Dust (IASFM, 1981)
Remembrances (IASFM, 1982)
Scarlet Snow (IASFM, 1982)
The Comet that Cried for its Mother (Amazing, 1984)